ROAD TO REDEMPTION

LOST & FOUND - BOOK THREE

MICHELLE DALTON

3 UMFANA PUBLISHERS

To those who deserve a second chance—and those who don't.

GLOSSARY

Augrabies – (ow-g(gravel sound in back of throat) r (roll the r) – ah-bees) or Augrabies Falls is a national park located in the Northern Cape Provence of South Africa.

Boet – (boot) brother

Boerieroll – (boo – rie – roll) a South African sausage (Boerwors) on a bread roll

Bokkie – (boh – ky) term of endearment, like dearie

Bobotie – (boh-bohti) a Malaysian South African dish

Bliksem/ed – (bluhk-sem) to hit

Bakkie – (bah-kie) ute or truck

Baas – (bahs) boss

Boesman – (boo-s-maahn) bushman

Crim/crims – criminals

Chookie – Colloquial for jail

Doos – (do - u - s) A very naughty Afrikaans curse word

Eina – (ay-nah) ouch

Gwaai – (g-why) colloquial term for a cigarette

Gabba – (gah, bah) close buddy, pal

Gevok – (ge fok) swear word—fucked

Grub – colloquial for food

Goedigge vok – (*g* (a gravely sound at the back of throat) oo-di*g* – uh f-oh-k) very naughty way of saying 'good grief'

Intombi – (In-toh-m-bi) Zulu for girl

Jy's a Kaffirs kind – A very derogatory term.

Jaapie – (Yaaapie)

Koeksisters – (kook-sisters) a deep fried sugary pastry

Kom Boessie – (k-ohm boosie) Come, Boosie.

Klein – (kl – ay – n) small

Larny – colloquial for fancy

Lossiepop – Term of endearment.

Larny – South African Slang for fancy or smart.

Liefie – (l-ee-f-ee) Lovie

Melktert – milk tart

Mevrou – (me -fr-ow) missus

Ne - (n-eh) hey

Nitro stick – Colloquial for Glow stick.

Nooigedacht – (n- oi – t – g (gravel sound)- eh – dah – gt) Name of a place meaning never thought.

Omie – (oh – mi) ouma – both mean grandmother, but are pronounced and spelled a little differently.

Oupa – (oh-pah) grandfather

Oakes – (oak-s) guys/men

Oom – (ooh-m) Uncle

Possie – (poh-sy) place

Piece job – colloquial term for part-time or casual job

Springhaas – (spru-ng-hahs) jackrabbit

Toe maar Boesie – (Too mahr Boosie) It's okay, Boesie.

Vokoff – (f-ohk off) F off

PROLOGUE

THE SCENT OF CHINA ROSES IN FULL BLOOM. SILKY SATIN skin beneath his fingertips ... Eyes the shade of Earth's richest soil sprinkled with hints of copper, and lips as red as ripe pomegranate, so sweet, so hot, so ...

The bus jolted and Raymond Le Roux found himself once again in the present.

———

"PENNY FOR YOUR THOUGHTS." Lullu giggled as she rode past Mina on horseback.

Mina twirled the rose between her index finger and thumb. She wasn't sure why, but she'd not been able to resist the bunch of lilac blooms when she'd visited town early this morning. They'd been her favourite, once upon a time.

Thoughtfully, she slipped the rose behind her right

ear and glanced at her daughter. Lullu flashed Mina one of her bright grins as she passed her a second time in the arena.

A soft ache trotted across her heart, as it always did and always would when her daughter smiled. She was the spitting image of her father.

Mina plucked the rose from her hair and dropped it to the ground.

1

WIPING A HAND DOWN HIS FACE AND ADJUSTING HIS jeans, Ray shook his head.

He focused on the ever-changing vista as the bus cruised down the narrow road. Here and there, they passed a donkey cart or a farm house. The ocean, to his left, ebbed and flowed, blue, pristine, and inviting. Holiday homes sat atop white dessert dunes with their matching whitewashed walls, thatched roofs, and fancy four-by-fours parked out the front.

A fellow inmate offered him a *gwaai*.

"You can't light up in here, *boet*, but thanks." He waved away the offer. The man simply shrugged and tucked the it behind his left ear.

The cigarette was tempting, the dream lingering.

The hunger for the long lost, of a time gone by, and the ever-demanding need for a hit fought for first place.

"Ssss." Ray sucked in a breath as his dream faded, leaving his nerve endings frayed and overwhelmed. A hit. Would the desire for oblivion ever go away?

For the first time in more than a decade, he was completely sober. Not even the acrid bitterness of nicotine had come close to his lips in over six months. He was dry, free of any sort of drug except his longing for her.

He could cope with the dreams of a distant, happier past, but the memories of what had robbed him of a life he could have led gnawed at him with poisoned, hungry fangs.

Ray was determined not to relapse, but only God knew how he would 'work through' the bottled up regret.

Drugs had kept him numb for so long. Actually feeling something was like being stung by a thousand hornets at once.

The constant stench of guilt hovered over him like a rotting corpse. Ray only just kept his head above the surface of the black hole he fought to keep from falling down once again.

He only had one person to blame: himself. He had so much to make up for—he would need three lifetimes to come anywhere close to redemption.

Ah ... the word reverberated through his soul. That was exactly where he was heading—Redemption. A farm for scum of the earth who'd been allowed a second chance.

He did not believe he deserved one, nor was he about to squander it.

The small Western Cape town of Tatensrope was the holiday possie for the rich, and the coast's gem— one of the few untouched landscapes left in his beloved country.

It was odd that this would be where a rehabilitation centre for crims was also located.

———

"Lullu! Will you please put on your hat?" Mina scolded her fair-haired daughter. The frown on the teenagers face deepened as she continued working her pony in the lunging ring.

"*Ja*, Ma," she replied as she slowed the Basotho gelding and beckoned to him.

Unlike Mina's darker olive skin and dark brown locks, her daughter took after her father's family in every respect, but for her eyes. Those, at least, she shared with her.

Mina glanced at her phone. The bus with ten new inmates was running late, as usual.

Africa time—a sense of things happening as and when they did—was something that Mina would never understand even if Africa was the blood coursing through her veins.

They'd also still not emailed her the paperwork— something about load shedding affecting their systems. Hopefully, printed copies of the new inmate register would accompany the driver.

"We're almost ready for Nationals." Lullu smiled as she strolled up to her with Boesman at her side. The pair were inseparable. Many a night, Mina would find her daughter asleep beside the horse.

Lullu had learnt to ride before she could walk thanks to one of Mina's old university buddies, who had a penchant for horses.

"Drina's trained you well," Mina said, "The nationals will be lucky to have you."

"We'll see." Her daughter said.

"Agh, look!" Lullu stopped and picked the rose up out of the dirt. "You dropped your flower." Lullu dusted off the waxy petals and handed it back to Mina.

A chill ran down her spine. "It's dying. Throw it away." Mina waved her hand as though to chase away a fly.

"Waste not, want not," her daughter mimicked words Mina would often throw at her. "I'll put it my bible and press it." She slipped the bloom into her shirt pocket. "*Kom*, Boessie." She tugged on her horse's halter, leading him off to the stables.

A soft wind blew from the inland, pushing against the humidity of the afternoon. A strange sensation snaked its way up Mina's spine as a memory from another life faded in and out of her mind's eye.

———

Ray pulled his bottle of soda from the pocket of the seat in front of him, unscrewed the lid, and gulped down the lukewarm, flat, sugary drink.

The psychiatrist in the dry-out ward of the prison had spent many sessions talking him through the choices he'd made. Doctor Eksteen had understood the trauma he'd had to deal with in silence. The day he'd shunned the girl he'd loved to protect her, and the devastation when his Ma had gotten ill and died. The anger and self-loathing that had eaten him alive from the inside out.

Once the drugs had finally left his system, Raymond had begun to understand the sacrifice his pa had made over the years, and that it was his pa who had saved him from a prison sentence. Six months rehab and six months on Redemption Farm before being released on parole. If he was lucky.

He had to make this work. It was his last chance at some semblance of a life, a life he would now devote to making up for all the evil he'd committed in the past.

The bus screeched to a halt. Through its large front window, the deep blue, froth-laced Atlantic greeted them as it curled, waved and receded. Out the side windows to his right, a number of stone cabins with grass roofs stood stacked in neat rows of three surrounded by what looked like a communal barbeque area and hall. This was paradise compared to the prison's rehab facility in Cape Town.

To the left of them, rows of solar panels drank up the sun's heat and beyond, warehouses where Raymond assumed the abalone was farmed and processed.

A ripple of fear rolled over him. He didn't want to stuff up, but what he knew of abalone was less than the dew found on a desert rose in the morning.

The farm was all about rehabilitation, but cleverly incorporated cheap labour too. The abalone, he assumed, was to keep the institution afloat.

On a hill in the distance, opposite the farm and cabins, stood a beautiful house designed in the same Cape Dutch-style as his pa's on Nooitgedacht wine farm. A deep emerald lawn and an immaculate garden, larger than the smaller one near the cabins, spread out around it with tall date palms reaching for the heavens. Ray squinted. Behind the abode stood a row of stables.

"Alright, Oakes! This is where you get off. Grab your bags and move it." The skinny weather-worn Afrikaans driver ordered.

Raymond gripped his duffel bag from the rack above. Inside, were the only possessions he had to his name—two pairs of denim pants, a pair of board shorts, three pairs of socks, four T-shirts, and his toiletries.

They all stumbled out of the bus and onto the soft white sand of Redemption Farm.

Raymond looked up, cupping his free hand over

his brow to shield his eyes from the sharp sun. A tall coloured man stood on a mound glaring down at them.

"My name is Benjamin Meintjies. You will address me as sir or Mr Meintjies. I am not your buddy, *gabba*, or mother," a deep, angry voice bellowed. "This is not a holiday resort!"

A young boy stood beside Mr. Meintjies as the driver handed him a sheet of paper. The burly man scanned it, looked up and gave each inmate a stern look. His beady eyes fell on Ray. A chill wrapped itself around his spine. Ben nodded, handed the paper to the boy and pointed toward the farm house on the hill before returning his attention to them.

"You are now at Redemption Farm. You're not here to waste my time or fuck around. This shit is real. For some reason, God, the judge, and the good owner of this place have decided you are worth their effort, and are entitled to a second chance." He fisted his hands and pinned them to his thighs. "I do not! You're all a bunch of washouts. A waste of space. So while you're here, you will follow my law and if you don't, I'll see you back behind bars before you can say sorry. And FY *blerrie* I ... that's where ninety percent of you will wind up anyway." His eyes travelled up and down the two rows of men and once again landed on Ray. Ben's words felt almost personally aimed at him.

Ray shook the feeling. He'd not fail—not this time. He had too much to make up for.

"Right, place your bags at your feet. Open them,

take a step back, and stand at attention ... and for those of you who don't know what attention is, you'd better figure it out, as in yesterday, or prepare to run the circumference of this farm which is a decent ten kilometres."

Ray dropped his bag and zipped it open before straightening his body, eyes forward and placing his arms rigidly beside his body. Memories of high school cadets flooded back. Every Monday morning, come rain or shine, their platoon would drill for an hour before school. They'd been the champs of the west coast.

"Name, inmate." Mr. Meintjies' face suddenly appeared before him, his nose a hair's breadth from Ray's.

"Raymond Le Roux, sir."

"Ah, army background. Well, haven't you fallen from grace." Ben smirked.

Raymond didn't bother to correct the man.

The man knelt on the ground and began to rifle through Ray's few possessions, not caring that clothes and toiletries fell into the dirt. He then proceeded to search Ray, "Spread your legs and arms." He barked as his hands slapped and grabbed their way around Ray's body. "Lift your shirt," he ordered, "Right, get your things. You're in cabin two." Mr Meintjies pointed toward the living quarters.

While it was obvious he was stern as a drill

sergeant to keep the men in line, there was a part of the man Ray recognised—an arrogant, power-hungry bully lurked just beneath the surface. Best he kept on the man's good side. Men like Mr. Meintjies could make life hell for blokes like Ray.

———

MINA'S HOUSE manager's son, Piet, trotted up to the office window. "Here, miss. The list from the driver. He said all their network is *gevok*."

"*Klein*, Piet! Mind your language," Mina chastised as she pushed open the large window and reached through the burglar bars for the sheet of paper.

"Sorry, miss. I mean, their stuff is broke." The boy looked to his feet. There were times he looked older than his sixteen years, but then, that was what a hard life did.

"What you mean is, their system is offline," she corrected him.

"Yes, miss. Offline." His cheeky grin irked Mina, but she took it with the good spirit it was intended.

"Thank you. Get back to work then. I'm sure Mr Meintjies needs help with the new inmates." She waved her hand in a way that told the boy he was dismissed.

Mina swivelled in her chair and placed the crumpled sheet of names on the desk beside her computer keyboard. She'd copy it into her computer so she had both a printed and digital copy.

Her eyes scanned the list of names and froze. Her heart stumbled and her breath caught. She reached, without looking away from the page, for her reading specs. She rarely wore the things.

Slipping the titanium frame on her face, she leaned forward, as though a closer look would prove her wrong.

Impossible!

Mina stood so fast her chair tipped over. Her vision blurred then righted as she gripped the paper, ripped the spectacles off, dropped them on her desk, and stormed outside. She only slowed her pace when she reached the edge of her garden. From here, she had a clear view of the camp and the inmates Ben was lining up and berating.

She knew his words were harsh and often cruel, and more than that—true, but with every intake, they managed to set two or three of her visitors on the right path. For Mina, that was enough. She didn't want to save the world, but that was no reason to give up on it.

Ben spoke their language; he'd been one of her first success stories. In all her years counselling criminals, she had come to the understanding that they knew no other language than the one Ben spoke. Hopefully, during their time at Redemption, she could teach them a new one. But that was not important now. What was important was finding the face which matched the name on the list.

Dear Lord—let it not be him!

Her mom, Grace, who still worked for Derek Le Roux had told her that Raymond had once again met the harsh hand of the law. But she'd never in her wildest dreams thought he'd end up here as one of her inmates.

Mina looked out over the dotted figures. She couldn't make out faces, but one in particular glowed like a nitro stick in the pitch dark. She knew it was him, even from this distance. The way he walked, stood ... fuck!

Perhaps it was a different Raymond Le Roux and not the boy who'd broken her heart and left her with a child to raise on her own. Well, to be fair, she'd never told him of ... oh, dear God. Mina didn't bother to spend any more time wondering.

She spun around on her heels and ran toward the stables.

Her world began to spin and her breath froze in her lungs.

After Raymond had shamed her in front of his friends all those years ago, she'd tried to understand, tried to catch a moment alone with him to ask him *why*? Why had he called her those names, rejected her, when only days earlier he'd loved her so thoroughly?

He'd been in a bad fight the day he'd broken up with her, and she'd suspected it was his cricket team laying down the laws about dating a *coloured* girl that had pushed him in to being so cruel.

But he'd shunned her at every turn, and called her a 'kaffirs kind'. That was the moment her heart had shattered in to a million pieces. Mina had vowed never to hand over her love, soul and loyalty to any man ever again.

Black dots clouded her vision and her legs began to cramp. Her throat constricted and her breathing shortened.

"Miss Mina, are you alright?" Becky, her house manager, ran up to Mina as she collapsed on the lawn, heaving. "I'll fetch your inhaler."

Becky turned and ran back in to the house.

"Find Lullu. I'll be okay." Mina huffed.

But Becky ignored her, shouting an order to cook in the kitchen, and returning a few moments later with her inhaler. She stood above Mina with the oddest smile on her face before landing on her knees and shaking the inhaler. The lack of oxygen must have been affecting Mina.

"Come. Open your mouth now." Becky brought the medicated inhaler up to Mina's lips.

"But Ma, how am I going to earn money? This isn't fair! I don't go anywhere near the inmates, and Ben always makes sure I'm with the hired workers in a different section of the farm," Lullu pleaded.

While Lullu always kept well clear of the camp, as was the rules, she did earn her pocket money by helping out with the abalone farming. She was always supervised and safe. But with things the way they were now, Mina did not want to take any chances.

For once, she wished she'd sent her daughter to a boarding school and not the local schoolhouse in town. The abalone nursery would be the one place she'd run in to her father.

"It's just for a while, Lullu, please. I have my reasons and I need you to trust me." Mina shook her inhaler and sucked in a puff of Ventolin. She felt a second asthmatic attack come on. She'd not had an attack in months. The medication eased the spasming tissue of her lungs and the action helped calm the crippling anxiety gripping her diaphragm.

"Agh. I can't wait till I'm eighteen." Lullu stomped her left foot, spun around, and stormed out of the kitchen.

At thirteen, she was proving to be a force of nature, Mina shuddered when she thought of the years to come. Lullu was generally a well-behaved child, but she had her ... father's stubborn streak and Mina's unwavering cheek, which made for a lethal combination.

"Don't worry, miss. Children will never understand

until the day they become parents," her cook soothed her.

Mina nodded. How true the woman's words were. How she had fought with her mom when Grace had discovered her and Ray were lovers. But in the end, her mother had been right, and Mina had paid a dear price.

2

Dusk spent beneath a large oak tree. He'd nipped some of his ma's sourdough bread and cheese, and a half bottle of Riesling from the fridge. Mina spread out a blanket and placed a bowl with dried fruit in its centre. Together, they sat watching the sunset.

The dipping shades of ochre and indigo brought her soft caramel skin to life. It was all he could do not to wrap her around him like a beautiful coat.

"One day, this will be ours." He spread his legs so that he could tuck her neatly between them and up against his chest. He wrapped his arms around her and leaned with his chin on her shoulder. The tips of her chocolate ponytail tickled his cheek.

"I can see our kids running between the vines, our parents sipping wine on the verandah while I cook up a big pot of oxtail." She tilted her head back, alerting Ray to the

fact that she wasn't wearing a bra beneath her spaghetti-strap top.

His hands slid beneath it and up her belly until they came to rest on her plump breasts and hard nipples.

Ray jerked awake. His body shuddered as the dream reminded his muscles and skin of the sweet love he'd made to her that evening. Sadly, the sensations melted away leaving him empty, alone, and desperately craving oblivion.

Regret stroked his twisted heart, and sweat soaked his pyjamas. Every muscle twitched anxiously; his gut clenched and twisted. All he wanted was a hit.

No! The folds of his arms and the areas between his toes ached for him to plunge a needle deep into them and sooth the yearning.

No! I am safe. I am stronger than my need! I am in control.

He swung his legs off the bed and concentrated on the cool concrete touching the soles of his feet. With shaking fingers, he pinched his earlobes then his cheeks—a distraction technique taught to them at rehab.

Slowly and with purpose, he inhaled, held his breath for the count of five, then exhaled. He repeated this while concentrating on the coolness seeping up from the floor and into his feet and legs. Eventually, the pain let go of his extremities and allowed him more movement.

What he needed was to run, but that was off-limits in the middle of the night.

He'd have to compromise.

Removing his drenched shirt, Raymond dropped to the floor and began with push-ups until his arms burned and his shoulders groaned. He twisted and did sit-ups. When his abdomen screamed mutiny, he once again twisted over and positioned his body in a plank. His roommate continued to snore in the bed on the opposite side of the small room, not in the least bit perturbed by Ray's physical therapy.

His night terrors were getting easier to cope with now—the longing and hunger for a hit subdued faster, but never truly went away.

The first weeks in the court-appointed rehabilitation centre had brought him closer to hell than anything he'd ever experienced in his entire life.

The pain, the anger, the bargaining, the *need* ... yes, that was something that would never leave him. The need, the all-consuming beast which clawed at its cage, demanding another high.

There were times he'd tried to scratch his skin from his body and others when he'd picked all the hairs of his eyebrows out with his fingers—this had landed him in a straightjacket. The hallucinations were worse. He saw his dead mother in every human he had contact with. One night, he'd fractured his left hand when he'd been convinced Benzile was attacking Mina. And then, it had stopped.

Thanks to a rather spectacular doctor and his team, Ray had made it through his personally inflicted hell and was discharged to Redemption Farm, armed with the mental tools that would help him cope. Plus the farm also offered three weekly AA meetings.

His legs and arms ached and cramped. Ray slowed down to shadow box bringing his heartrate and breathing under control.

Grabbing his towel and toiletries, he decided to hit the shower before everyone woke up. Raymond padded softly across the courtyard to the communal bathroom when movement in the distance, beyond the buildings and closer to the warehouses, caused him to stop.

It was not quite dawn but the half-moon shed enough light for him to see where he was going. Ray slipped into the shadows as he squinted. Someone stood flashing a light out toward the ocean. A light flashed back. Ray could only see an arm, the rest of the person hid behind a retaining wall. Ray held his breath, he was a mere meter or two from whoever this was. The light flashed again. The arm was skinny, like that of a child, with a thick keloid scar wrapped around it like a snake.

A crow cawed from a nearby tree, and the figure stepped forward. Ray ducked and froze. It was probably the night guard signalling the coast guard. He'd read somewhere that breeding farms worked in conjunction with conservation West Coast to protect the sea life. But his instincts told him to stay out of sight regardless.

Ray re-entered the room as his alarm buzzed on the table beside him. It was the dawn of a new day— the first of his new life and he was ready for it.

"Hey Cyril, it's time to get up, man," he called to his roomie, who raised a hand and waved him away.

Showered and dressed in his work uniform, which consisted of a pair of khaki cargo pants, work boots, and a button-up shirt with a starched collar and the Redemption Farm logo embroidered on its pocket, Ray followed the inmates to the mess hall for breakfast.

"Right, you will find a list pinned to the notice board at the back of the hall. This will tell you where you're allocated to work for the week. On the table beneath, you'll find some maps of the farm. Take one each and use it to navigate your way around the place. This means there is no excuse not to be on time." Mr Meintjies welcomed them with his demands. "Lunch is at twelve-thirty sharp, after which you will all remain in the hall to attend your first group therapy session," he informed them before turning on his heel and leaving them to their meals.

Ray finished his porridge then went to check the list and collect a map. According to the allocations, his job for the week would be to shadow one of the workers in checking that the environment for growing abalone was perfect.

Collecting a printed sheet from the pile on the

table below the board, Ray turned and made his way out.

Stepping into the sticky humidity from the mess-hall, Ray turned his map this way and that, he needed to go to building 2A. Before lay the ocean, behind him the dining hall and he should...

A distant whinny caused him to stop and look up. The house was farther away from where he stood compared to their compound, but he could still make out the form of a young girl sitting astride a pony at the edge of the hill which met the beach. Long blond hair twisted and fluttered in the ocean breeze as she curled her bare legs and feet around the horse's belly.

"Le Roux! You've no business standing around. Move your *blerrie* arse or start running," Ben bellowed from the entrance of a nearby building.

"Yes, sir." Raymond nodded and returned to finding building 2A.

He glanced back. The girl was gone, but not the strange sense of recognition which had settled in his centre at the sight of her.

———

THE SIREN FOR LUNCH SOUNDED. It reminded Ray of a school lockdown drill. That was yonks ago. A time when he'd had dreams and ... love. Ray shook the memories from his head as he removed his work gloves and placed them with his protective goggles, apron, and gumboots in their allocated area. He'd spent the first hour in a room behind a desk being educated on what abalone was, and how Redemption artificially bred the much sought-after sea snail both for sale across the globe and to reintroduce to the ocean.

He'd sat through what he'd thought was a helluva interesting lecture on how a man up in Gauteng had found a way to create real seawater. Who'd have thought it was so intricate and how important the foam formed on the surface of the ocean was to marine life? And this man had managed to replicate it to perfection.

Once the lecture was done, he'd been taken to the warehouse and ordered to clean tanks. While the task was menial, Ray had relished the numbing actions of scrubbing, rinsing, and repeating.

After pushing his socked feet into his work boots, he washed his hands and made his way out the back entrance toward the mess hall. His stomach growled. He was looking forward to some good nosh.

"Definitely not chookie grub, eh." Cyril lifted his plate and licked. Ray smiled, stood, and grabbed his tray.

Ray scraped the few leftovers from his meal of fish fingers, mashed potatoes, and green beans into the bin before waiting in line to rinse his plate then place it in the industrial-sized dishwasher.

An elbow nudged him in his back. "I hear we gotta

sit through one of those 'share your feelings' sessions now."

A man Ray judged to be at least twenty years his senior with missing front teeth and sporting a grey beard, wearing a blue-knitted beanie and matching uniform said to Ray. In the old days, Ray would have held out his hand and introduced himself, but these days, he felt no need to make friends.

Ray simply nodded.

He'd taken notice when Ben had informed them of the group therapy session after lunch. He wouldn't admit it to the other inmates, but he was looking forward to it. He *needed* it.

A woman with dreadlocks hanging halfway down her back and skin as dark as ebony walked into the mess hall. She made her way to the front with a confident strut and a laptop bag in her left hand.

Ray looked to his feet in shame. He owed so many so much. Mere months ago, he'd have reacted like the total asshole he'd allowed himself to become. He'd have refused to be lectured by a black person; today, he couldn't wait to share his trials with anyone willing to listen.

"Please bring your chairs and gather around." She placed the bag on the podium then stood before it, beckoning to them with long, lithe arms jingling with bracelets and beads. Her very English accent caused most of the men to do a double take.

Ray stood and picked up his chair as Mr. Meintjies

rushed in and headed straight for the woman. A look of concern was painted across his face. Ray didn't move but watched as they had a soft, brisk exchange before he stormed back out.

———

"No, you don't understand, I cannot accommodate this inmate." Mina tried to explain to the woman on the other end of the line.

"But Miss van der Westhuizen, according to our contract, unless the inmate has re-offended or broken the terms of his parole you are obliged to keep him on until he completes the six-month term. Has he done this?"

"No." Mina exhaled.

"Then I don't understand what the issue is. You have never had a problem before."

Mina's wedge caught in a dip on her lawn an she angrily kicked off the shoes she'd worn to match her crème culottes and baby-blue cotton blouse. She combed frustrated fingers through her blow-dried shoulder-length hair, her signet ring catching on a few strands.

Eina!

She spun around on her heel and froze. It was one of the windier spring days on the west coast, and her garden lay green and wind-strewn around her. Ben

Meintjies was making his way up the hill toward her. His eyes were dark, his frown serious.

Mina didn't want him ... or anyone, for that matter, to know of her past with Raymond Le Roux.

"Fine. I'll make it work," she blurted and hung up.

"What's that about?" He nodded toward the phone in her hand as he came to stand beside her.

Ben Meintjies, an ex-prison guard turned drug smuggler turned rehabilitated farm manager, was built like a brick shithouse and had the personality to match.

"Nothing. How's the new group settling in?" Mina clasped her hands behind her back.

"Fine, but I'm left wondering why my boss didn't give me a heads up you weren't leading this group's counselling session." The black of his gaze deepened.

"I have too much on my plate at the moment." She slipped her phone into her back pocket.

Ben cocked his head considering her for a moment. She knew he didn't buy it. She also knew the man held a flame for her, and had held it since the day she'd hired him. She did not need him knowing about her past with Raymond Le Roux.

"The inmates? Are they grasping all the new rules, and ideas around our farming methods?"

"*Ja*, they're settling in okay. This bunch are a bit more chilled than our previous group. By the way, Drikus sent me a text. He's settled in well with the conservation group in Augrabies."

"That's great news. It's not easy for the older ones to change their ways," Mina replied as they strolled toward her house.

"So, am I allowed to ask why you're not presenting the therapy session? You've never missed one before."

Mina swallowed hard. " I told you, I'm really busy." She didn't look at him. "I've known Vestra since our university days. She's great. You know that. I'd prefer she take over this group so I can concentrate on—other things."

"Hey." He grabbed her hand and turned her to face him, "What is going on? You've been out of sorts of late. Is it Lullu's comp ... or something else?" A shadow crossed his face.

Mina gently pulled her hand from his. Ben used any excuse to try and get close to her, and while she respected him greatly as a man and a manager, she'd never feel more or want him to believe there was hope for a relationship between them. She'd told him this many times over.

"Yeah. The vaulting tournaments are getting tougher. She's dealing great with the stress, but me? I poop myself every time she gets on that horse's back." Mina half-lied.

"She's a bright one that girl of yours, I doubt you have little to worry about. Well. I need to get back. You know where to find me if you need a shoulder." Ben tucked his hands in his pockets, his expression hooded.

Mina smiled and watched him walk back to the inmate camp.

She'd have to control of the situation from afar. Vestra had been itching to take the lead on one of the groups, and now had been as good a time as any. There were many other things demanding Mina's attention. The demand for abalone had increased and all the farms on the west coast were on high alert after poachers had hit three of them in as many weeks. She'd also not lied about the increase in difficulty of her daughter's vaulting competitions either. But mainly she did not want to run into Ray.

Mina made her way back to her study.

Swivelling in her chair, she glanced out of the window. She'd get them through this without a fuss. She had to. She couldn't send Ray away—that much was clear.

Her heart lurched as her thoughts drifted back to a time when she considered herself innocent, naïve and completely in love.

Sunlight filtered through the leaves of the old oak, dappling her skin in patches of gold. It highlighted his mop of milky-white curls which hugged those bright blue eyes.

"I could stare at you forever." His words caressed her heart.

"We have to go soon. My mom will wonder where I am," she replied as she stroked his face.

Ray shifted slightly where he lay snug and warm

between her legs. It was late afternoon and they'd managed to escape after rushing through their chores.

Their hidden place was rarely visited by others, all the way down the bottom of the vineyard at Nooitgedagt. A small clump of old oaks and the odd willow hugged the crystal waters of a stream which separated Nooitgedagt from the farm next door.

"Six more months and I'll be done with school." He leaned forward and stroked her cheeks and neck with his hungry lips.

"And then what, Ray? What will that change?" She loved him so much it hurt, but she was sixteen and coloured. Unless they left the country, which she could never do, was there a future for them? Sure, apartheid was no more—but that did not mean prejudice had died overnight.

"And then to hell with everyone. I am my father's heir."

"So?" she snapped.

"You are mine!"

"And you're mine."

She took his hand and slipped it between her legs then reached for him. He reacted instantly to her touch growing hard where he lay naked and beautiful between her legs.

Lifting slightly, he perched his tip against her entrance, "You will always be mine, Mina van der Westhuizen, and no one can change that!"

He slid inside her.

Mina's stomach flipped, and the spot between her legs grew moist and hot at the memory of a time when her life was bright with promise and filled with love. What an absolute fool she'd been to believe any of it. Some part of her still believed his broken promises, but the rejected single mother inside of her raged against the memories and feelings his presence had reawakened.

3

DEREK LE ROUX SAT DOWN AT HIS KITCHEN TABLE, A white envelope clasped in his trembling hands. It had no sender details, but he recognised the writing. How could he not?

Inhaling deeply, he grabbed the unused butter knife beside his breakfast plate and slid it inside the corner, slicing open the lip of the envelope. This was the first time he'd heard from his son since his sentencing more than six months ago. And according to his calendar, Ray had completed his first week at the farm.

A tremble moved from his hands to the tips of his fingers as he pealed open the single-page letter.

Pa.

I need to say so much. But every time I try to, I have no words. There are no justifications to pardon a man like me. I don't deserve forgiveness. I will try not ask for forgiveness, but to say sorry.

Sorry I disappointed you. Sorry I destroyed your trust in me. Sorry I ruined your good name.

Derek placed the letter face down on the table and bit back the wave of emotion threatening to overwhelm him. Wiping tears from his eyes with the back of his hands, he returned to reading.

I owe so many so much. After all, sorry is just a word, but I don't know how else to convey my unrelenting grief over what I have done. Shelly—I treated her and Thomas like shit. But more than that, I hurt someone who meant more to me than my own life. I threw her away like a used dish rag. I know why I did it, not that it excuses my actions, but I owe her a better explanation. And you. I ruined everything you worked so hard for. My selfish actions almost got you killed. Ma died thinking I was a failure ...

My self-hatred destroyed so much that was good. Perhaps someday I'll stop being a coward.

I've been given one last chance. I vow not to waste it. Redemption Farm is beautiful. I promise not to let you down again.

A flicker of hope lit Derek's heart. When he'd testified for his son, he'd had a word with the magistrate beforehand. Smittie was an old friend; he'd asked the man to make sure Ray was sent to Redemption Farm. He knew beyond a doubt that it was his son's last chance for healing, for facing the truth and maybe leading a better life.

He turned in his chair and called out, "Grace!"

It was time to let Mina's mother know what he'd planned.

———

"MOMMY?"

A gentle voice drifted across the warm breeze and stirred the grass.

Mina pushed up from where she lay dressed in a pair of denim shorts, sans T-shirt. Ray lay beside her, his birthday suit reflecting the gold of the sun he bathed in.

Mommy!"

Mina shot straight up from where she lay on her double bed. Rubbing her eyes, she yawned then gasped when she found Lullu sitting at the foot of her bed, eyes wide, cheeks flushed.

"Were you dreaming of my dad?" Lullu, dressed and ready for school, asked.

"Wha—why ... erm, no!"

"You were moaning weirdly. Who's Ray then?" Lullu dropped her head and glanced at her through wispy black lashes.

Mina had long ago sat down and explained to Lullu that her father was gone. She'd never bothered asking much about him and Mina had assumed that Derek le Roux was enough of a male figure in her daughter's life—but this!

Mina swallowed hard.

"It must have been a nightmare." She reached out and tucked a loose strand of sunshine behind her daughter's ear.

"Are you still going to watch me train this afternoon before I go to help out with the harvesting?"

Mina wiped a shaking hand down her face. Thank goodness Lullu hadn't asked more questions. Mina turned and dropped her bare feet to the floor as she glanced at the clock on her bedside table. Six-thirty a.m.

"I've told you, no going down to the warehouses for the time being."

"Maaa." Lullu dragged out the word, balling her small, strong fists. "There's a blanket I want to get Boesman, and I need to work if I want to afford it."

"I'll buy it for you." Mina sighed. "Besides, you can help Becky out around the house."

"Agh. I hate housework."

"Well, it'll have to do for now."

"I don't get it. Why won't you just tell me why?" Her daughter pleaded.

"Because I've decided it's no place for a young woman, and that's what you almost are." Mina lied.

"So what, a small girl is safer?"

"Agh, Lullu, it's just..." Goodness this was harder than she imagined. Where were the days when her little girl simply believed and accepted everything Mina told her?

"Did I make a mistake? What aren't you telling me?

I'm one of the best at harvesting, and you know it." Lullu stomped her foot.

"You'll just have to pretend you're a big girl and that you understand for now. Besides, I could do with one of those awesome milkshakes at the coffee shop." She proffered her daughter a smile, hoping her attempt at a bribe worked.

"Since when do you like milkshakes?" Lullu giggled.

"Since today." Mina reached forward and grabbed her daughter, pulling the lanky-limbed teen into her arms. She promptly began to tickle her.

"Sto-o-op." Lullu laughed as she twisted around, trying to grip the hand causing her laughing fit. "I'm still upset. But a milkshake might fix it … a little." She squinted at Mina through her index finger and thumb to indicate what she meant.

"Good. I need to shower and get dressed." Mina sighed inwardly. The distraction had worked this time, but Mina knew it would not keep for long. Lullu was a perfectly sculpted creature who owned equal parts of the good and bad in both her and Ray, and unfortunately, every ounce of their combined stubbornness too.

"School first, and this afternoon after practice, it'll be you, me, and the shops. But first you need to catch that bus or you'll be late." She patted her daughter's bottom as the girl stood.

———

WITH LULLU OFF at school and her morning planned, Mina sat at her desk, a steaming cup of coffee beside her.

She'd pushed open her large windows and was enjoying the soft sea breeze drifting in. She leaned back in her chair and sighed. The dreams she'd had every night since Ray's arrival **(Check time line!)** stayed with her during her days. His touch, his smell— goodness, she had to find a way to forget. Life was a funny thing. Just when you thought you had it sorted it'd always throw the next curveball.

"Miss! Miss!" Klein Piet ran up to her window, eyes wide and lips pale.

"What now?" Mina rose.

"There's *groot kak* ..."

A bucket of imaginary ice tipped over Mina's head.

"Sorry, I mean big shit ... agh, miss, I don't know the words, but Baas Ben, he sent me to fetch you 'cause they broke into warehouse five." The young boy huffed as he leaned forward, resting his hands on his knees. His hazel eyes watched her intently. He had a way of making her feel uncomfortable even though he'd never given her reason to doubt him.

Mina gripped her cell phone from her desk. "Tell Ben I'm coming," she said, and hastily made her way down to the warehouses. Shit a brick! This close to harvesting, she prayed the Abalone were okay. She had insurance on her crop, but fuck sake it still cost to lose or suffer damage.

"God damn bloody poachers!" she muttered as she stomped down the slate-paved steps of her garden, past the inmates' living quarters, and toward the farthest warehouse numbered five, where abalone was prepared for harvesting or repatriation to the ocean beds.

Poaching was one of Africa's greatest enemies. It stole, slaughtered, and destroyed without mercy, all for the gain of those who sat high and mighty in their glass towers believing myths of what ground-up horns and shells could provide.

In all her years of having owned Redemption, they had only ever once experienced trouble. She'd thought the security she'd had installed after a heads up from West Coast Conservation last year would have been enough—apparently not.

Huffing, she tapped the phone screen and dialled the local conservation trooper's number. "Marnus!" she blurted into the receiver when he answered.

"I heard. Ben called. We're on our way. I've let Abbe at the police station know too."

"Thanks. See you soon," she replied gratefully and tucked her phone into her pocket as she rounded the western corner of the warehouse, pushed past a few inmates who greeted her solemnly, and entered.

Her heart crashed to the concrete floor beneath her feet. Fuck it was worse than bad... it was...

"They took half our crop." Ben came to stand beside her.

"And the remaining abalone—are they damaged?"

"No. Simon heard a ruckus and disturbed them." He nodded toward one of her permanent staff. "We saved one more batch they left on the beach."

Mina looked up. Ben's face was hard, his eyes cold, and he did not look back at her.

"And what about the alarm? Why didn't it go off?" Mina turned and walked to the keypad beside the door.

"Tampered with. Whoever did it knew how to get around this specific system." Ben grunted.

"What? But there's supposed to be a failsafe for that. The security company had better have answers." Mina placed her balled fists on her hips.

"You'll need to take that up with them. Maybe think of hiring a new group altogether," he muttered, not looking at her, but focusing on the empty benches where once, baths full of adult abalone had sat.

"This group—are there any of them you suspect?" Mina whispered.

Ben sighed as he rubbed his eyes with a large calloused thumb and index finger. "Hard to say. They've been here for around a week. Doubt that'd be enough time, but I'd not discount it."

He turned his dark gaze on her. "And you. You've read their files ..." He paused as though to think on his next words. "Do you suspect anyone?"

Mina's insides flipped. Was Ray capable? And had Ben made the connection?

She shook her head. "No." She'd contact Cape Prisons for more background on them all.

Ben didn't reply, his eyebrow cocking.

Voices and footsteps drew their attention as Marnus, the local conservation trooper, and Sergeant Abbe Deloise stepped in to the warehouse.

———

"It's obvious they used a skiff. The trawler probably sat anchored on the far end of the bay." Abbe pointed to drag marks left in the soft white sand of the beach edging the abalone warehouses. "They must have come in on the tide."

Mina swallowed hard. "Why now? We've been here for years—not a single issue." Lifting her hand to her brow, she gazed out over the cerulean waters. It was a beautiful day. The ocean lay flat as a lake, the sun bright and bold. "We have state-of-the-art security."

"*Ja*, they made quick work of that. I'll have to speak to your security company, employees and inmates. Also, give me the numbers for the delivery companies that are made to the farm—it could be anyone. I'll need everything you can give me on past inmates, especially those who were not able to complete the program," Abbe requested as she turned around and walked toward the area which had sustained the most damage. All the troughs which had once held adult Abalone were gone leaving a gaping emptiness in the benches specialy built to hold them.

Mina followed Abbe, her hopes dashed and her mind reeling when she noticed a hooded expression flash across the sergeant's face as she watched Ben Meintjies hand out orders at the far end of the building.

"He's trustworthy," Mina blurted. feeling suddenly defensive.

"Is he?" Abbe glanced at her. "Mina, at this stage, I'm not sure who is who anymore. With state officials dipping their hands into any pocket they want"—her glance bounced from Ben to Marnus and back to Mina —"and corruption using the old apartheid excuse, you need to be careful. Poaching on the west coast has increased in the last months. This new bunch have no regard for life and are connected to some powerful people."

A shudder snaked its way down Mina's spine. "I will, but I also vouch for all my people."

Abbe simply shrugged and walked toward Ben.

Mina sighed deeply as she gripped her phone to call her security company. She scrolled through the numbers as she strolled back to the house. She wanted an explanation, and they'd have to come out and replace the keypad. Perhaps a call to Derek? His son-in-law was an Interpol agent who'd busted the child-trafficking ring down in Cape Town—perhaps he could help?

Next call was her insurance, and then ...

"Mina?" A voice that hadn't changed a bit over the years settled like a bonfire in her centre. He could still turn her insides to mush. Mina froze, looked up, and swallowed hard.

"Ray." Her reply was a mere whisper as her gaze got caught in his astonished baby blues.

"Wh—how ...?"

Gathering all her strength, Mina raised her trembling hand, glancing past him to make sure Ben and everyone else were nowhere near them. "Not now. No one can know."

It was all she could muster.

"But—"

"Not now!" she hissed. "Get to the mess hall," she ordered and took off like a bolt toward the house. Every nerve fibre, cell, and shard of what was once her heart dug into her shattered soul, electrifying her body. Her chest throbbed and her lungs froze as she hurried toward the safety of her home. She really had to learn to carry her asthma pump around with her.

4

RAY STOOD, HIS LIMBS FROZEN AS SHE STRODE AWAY, HER back ramrod straight, fists clenched. She was shocked, but her eyes had told him she was not surprised.

His blood raced along the corridors of his body and his heart throbbed a painful staccato, begging for release from its cage.

She was as beautiful as she'd been on the day he'd broken her heart. The scent of China roses invaded his memories. His hands clenched open and shut and his gut churned with a need that threatened to override his will.

His Mina was as beautiful as ever. But the years sat etched along the corners of her eyes and mouth. In the few moments life had allowed him to look at her, anger, fear, and, right in the very depths of her gaze, a shattered love had shone bright like the warning flicker of a lighthouse lamp. All had fought for first place; none had won.

He was the storm who'd destroyed her precious innocence, and for that, there was no going back.

Forcing a hard breath in to his lungs, he held on to the affirmation taught to him at rehab.

I am safe. I am stronger than my need! I am in control.

What in all the heavens was she doing here? And why didn't she want anyone to know about them?

"Le Roux! What the fuck are you just standing around for? Better days! Move your arse." Ben's voice thundered, splintering his thoughts. The burly man came to stand beside him. "I know you were involved with that crooked son of a bitch down in Constantia. The courts let your involvement in kid smuggling go … just remember I'm watching you." He poked a stubby finger into Ray's chest. "Now get a move on."

Ray bit back the anger at Ben's assumption. He simply nodded as the man walked off. He wouldn't bother defending himself or the fact that his involvement had been drug-related. He was a shit, but he'd never harm a kid. Never!

Letting go of the air which had turned to ice in his lungs, Ray forced his limbs to move, and with effort, made his way to the hall alongside the other inmates. He'd heard about the break-in and, like the others, was preparing for an interrogation and possible accusations over being involved. Ray didn't care.

His mind was riddled with questions, confusion,

pain, and need. *Just one,* the voice begged. *No!* He beat it back.

"Bro. Do you think one of us *oakes* are involved?" Cyril, his roommate, whispered as they made their way to the chairs and tables in the mess hall. "I think it's that Jaapie bloke from cabin three. He's always sniffing around asking questions."

Ray shrugged and pulled out a chair and sat. The memory of his first night, and the person flashing a torch, resurfaced. He wasn't going to mention it. Snitches were bitches.

Folding his arms across his chest, he continued to concentrate on his breathing, fighting the need not only for a hit, but to stand up and run after the only woman he'd ever loved.

Ray barely noticed Ben show a police woman and another man dressed in a khaki uniform to the front of the hall.

"This is Sergeant Abbe Deloise. She and Ranger Marnus Faldela are investigating last night's break-in. You will co-operate. You will watch yourself. If I hear that you're a problem, a simple phone call is all it takes to end your time here," Ben bellowed across the hall, but Ray barely took notice as the man continued to explain that each of them would be questioned individually and that no one was to leave the hall until they were done.

The voices and faces around Raymond blurred into white noise as memories long buried beneath a haze of narcotics, anger, and pain surfaced like a demon corpse clawing its way from a watery grave to haunt and remind him of what he'd thrown away.

"You know we're not supposed to mix." Karl, the cricket captain, pushed him in to a corner of the cloakroom. The rest of the team surrounded the pair. Their eyes were dark and filled with hatred, aimed at him.

"But we're all friends," a seventeen-year-old Ray waved a hand at the team who was made up of white, coloured, and Xhosa—boys who had been allowed into their once only-white school when the walls of segregation had finally crumbled, but not disappeared.

"But we don't touch one another's women!" Benzile, their best fielder, spat at him.

"Leave her or pay for your actions," Jantjie called out.

Karl's fist gripped Ray's collar roughly. "You heard the boys. Leave her. If it's a fuck you need, Anke De Waal is always willing."

"No. I love her! It shouldn't be an issue. You can do what you want to me ..."

"And what do you think we'll do to her?" Benzile's voice sliced across Ray's heart.

He tried to fight back, but one against twelve strapping, angry, bitter lads was never meant to be a fair match ...

"Raymond ..."

A distant voice and someone's hand on his shoulder dragged Ray from the depths of his nightmarish memory.

"Hey bro, you're up." Cyril pointed to the man in

khaki waving for him to follow. "By the way, probably best not to mention my midnight smoking excursions." He winked.

Ray nodded. They weren't allowed to smoke in their cabins. Why Cyril saw his nightly *gwaai* breaks as an issue only he knew. It wasn't like he was the only one taking them. Probably nerves. They all hated the police.

Ray wiped sweaty palms down the front of his pants and walked up to where the ranger stood waiting to escort him to his interrogation.

I am safe. I am stronger than my need! I am in control.

———

THE EVENING WAS COOL. Ray sat on a plastic garden chair outside of his room, pen and paper in hand as her tried to enjoy the soft hum of crickets as the sky morphed from scarlet to deep indigo. He opened the pen the writing pad. They had access to computers, but Ray didn't have an email account and hadn't owned a phone since his last arrest.

He rather enjoyed the feel of the hand gliding across the sheet as he penned a new letter to his pa. Another memory from a different life popped into his head.

He'd loved journaling and had written many poems in his youth. He'd loved reading too...

It'd been a boiling-hot day, the heat following the moist

breeze into the night when he'd walked out to their oak tree. "Thought I'd find you here."

Moonlight cast a silver blanket across Mina's bare shoulders where she sat wrapped in only a blanket, her hair bundled up in a mess atop her head.

"Couldn't sleep either?" She smiled.

He sat down beside her and tucked her beneath his arm as he paged to his favourite poem and read. "Tyger, Tyger, burning bright ..."

He'd not picked up a book of poetry in yonks.

Shit, he'd wasted so many years. If only he'd been more of a man, if only ...

Three days had flown by since his run-in with Mina, and he'd not heard a word from her, not even a whisper. Not that he deserved any sort of explanation from her, but the thought that she lived only a few hundred metres from where he now lived, ate at him daily.

He'd figured out she was the owner of Redemption Farm and that she was usually more involved with the inmates. In his conversation with the counsellor, he was told she'd taken a step back to deal with the break-in, but Ray knew better, and the thought irked him.

She must hate him, and he couldn't blame her, but it still hurt to think that he'd turned the most beautiful soul in his life to a bitter woman.

Too bitter to involve herself in the work she was apparently passionate about, but too proud to make him leave, he assumed, as he was still here.

Ray blocked out his thoughts. Perhaps his father would understand? It was time to tell him what had happened so long ago to turn his son into the monster Ray had become.

Pa,

I'm not sure how to word this, and please know that I am not angry. Confused, yes. Deserving of all the hurt coming my way, absolutely, but not angry.

Grace still runs the house at Nooitgedacht, I take it? Did you know about Mina ...

Ray scratched out her name. She'd made it clear she wanted no one to know, and their mail was read and checked before it was sent out.

Did you know?

He wrote instead.

I don't blame you for never telling me.

There was a robbery here. Everyone is okay, but half the abalone harvest was taken. This was when I found out. God, Pa, beauty has no age limit! Is that inappropriate? I don't care. It's time to explain what happened. Not that it will ever excuse any of the crimes I've committed over the last years, but I promise to spend the rest of my life fixing it all.

It was the last game of the season just before mock exams for matric started ...

Ray handed the unsealed envelope to Mr. Meintjies who collected the mail the inmates wanted posted.

Mr. meintjies gave him a cold stare as he pulled the letter out and began to read it in front of Ray.

Ray didn't budge. Barley breathed as he fought his anger.

"Aw, isn't it just a shame how all you poor fuckers always get to blame someone else for your bullshit?" He tucked the letter back into the envelope and sealed it.

He'd get his own back and Mr. Meintjies would pay for his condescending shit, but not today.

Mr. Meintjies had been present during the interviews with the police, apparently to represent the inmates, but Ray had gotten a different vibe—he wasn't sure about it yet, but there was something about the man that didn't bode well with Ray. Anyhow, who was he to question anyone after all the wrong he'd committed?

"Will you be fine with me taking a run along the strand this afternoon, sir?" He controlled the tone of his voice. To allow Mr. Meintjies to know he'd pushed his buttons would be a grave mistake.

"Tired of the road to the gate and back?" Mr. Meintjies smirked.

"No, I just need a harder workout and the sand will do that."

He nodded. "And because I am such a magnanimous soul, you can clean out the toilets for me granting you that favour."

Ray clenched his fists and gritted his jaw, nodding, "Yes Sir."

Ray made his way back to the bungalow. Fucking

Ben Meintjies was just like Karl—a bully with the upper hand. Ray leaned with his palms flat against the outside wall of his cabin and breathed.

Run, he needed to run.

I am safe. I am stronger than my need! I am in control.

Ray straightened and marched inside, grabbed his trainers and a pair of socks.

The sun dazzled the ocean as the it displayed its beauty in the form of crimson and orange sprites surfing the waves. Ray was halfway back to the beach entrance which led up to the warehouses and inmate living area. With his run almost complete, he relished the burn in his thighs and calves. He controlled his breathing and smiled as the ocean breeze cooled the sweat drenching his torso. He was undeservedly blessed.

A horse's soft nicker caused him to look left. High up on a grass-covered dune stood the same bronze horse and on its back, a girl with long milky hair and a broad smile. Ray stumbled in the sand then regained his balance. His legs slowed to a stop as his mind digested the sight. For the slightest moment, he could have sworn he knew her. Some part of him recognised something about her.

The way she looked at him ... they'd never met before—that he was sure of.

A second figure joined the girl.

Mina!

A shocked expression contorted her face. She

uttered a few words to the girl who then tugged on the reins and rode off.

Mina remained staring down at him. He continued staring up. The world around them faded, and the slightest sliver of hope sparkled in the depths of Ray's heart.

As quickly as she'd appeared, Mina turned and walked away. Ray wiped a trembling hand down his face. That girl—why did he feel so connected to her? A second thought followed short on the first; surely ... no, impossible. His father would never keep that a secret from him. Would he?

Ray took off down the beach at a faster, harder pace. Could the girl be the reason why Mina was keeping him at a distance?

He needed to write to Pa. He could barely handle the fact Mina lived in such close proximity ... but he had to be certain of the girl or he'd snap.

Ray slowed his pace and came to a stop. He turned to face the setting sun over the ocean, gripping his sides with both hands as he fought to calm his mind and his breathing. The distant waning warmth cupped his thoughts and carried him back to a dusk long ago.

"Ray, please. I just need you to listen," Mina had begged him.

She'd come looking for him in the storeroom. He couldn't look at her; every time he did, his resolve melted and that would lead to her being harmed.

"Vokoff, Mina! We've had our fun. Time to move on." He leaned with his head against the damp inner walls of the store, gritting his teeth, hating himself and fighting back the urge to pull her into him and kiss away all the hurt he'd caused. Instead, he reached into his pocket and pulled out the flake of oblivion he'd procured on the corner after school. He popped it beneath his tongue and allowed the drug to take hold.

"Ray, please. I need to tell you ..."

He pushed away from the wall and, mustering all his self-loathing and bitterness, spat, "Jy's a Kaffirs kind. Don't ever come near me again!"

He watched as the words shattered the soul of the girl he loved. Her devastation pushed the knife deeper into his bleeding heart and snuffed whatever light had dared to burn in its centre.

Ray's body shuddered as his memories tore at his conscience. Had she possibly been trying to tell him she was pregnant? Oh dear God! That would have changed everything.

A wave crashed and ran to his feet, splashing over his trainers and up his legs. The briny water was cold compared to the warmth in the air and tugged Ray back to the present.

Regret was his worst enemy, and he had so much of this. He should have fought harder, gone to his pa and ma; they would have helped him keep Mina safe. But back then he'd been too much of a coward to make a stronger stance and had lost everything.

Even if that beauty on the back of the horse was his, she was better off without him.

Twisting abruptly in the sand, Ray made his way up to his quarters. The guys had lit a bonfire in the pit and were sitting around, chatting and enjoying a well-known easy meal.

"Hey bro, there's a *boerieroll* with your name on it." Cyril waved him over.

Ray nodded and shook off the ghosts of his past as he sat on the wooden bench, accepting the sausage on a bread roll. "Thanks."

This was where he now belonged—amongst the riff-raff of society, because that was what he had chosen to become. He had no rights.

I am safe. I am stronger than my need! I am in control.

It did no one any good to remain stuck in his past; that would only lead him down the cliff. Perhaps he could ask Vestra if she was open for one-on-one counselling? He needed an ear, guidance, and someone to catch him should he fall.

"There's a letter on your bed, by the way. Mr Meintjies dropped it off soon after you went for your run," Cyril added.

Ray's stomach flipped and he swallowed his bite of food, which dropped like lead into his stomach.

5

"Ma, you need to talk him out of it." Mina paced with her phone against her ear. Derek had called half an hour before, letting her know he was bringing her mom for a visit and that he wanted to see Raymond.

"*Bokkie*, I can't. We all knew this day would come. I didn't think it'd be like this but ... look, Derek has a right to visit his son and Raymond to receive visitors, just like all your other inmates." Her mother's voice stern yet loving drifted into her ear.

"Please, I can't have anyone here know about me and Ray. Lullu has no idea, and I'd prefer to keep it that way," Mina pleaded.

"You haven't told her?"

"I don't have to. I won't upend my daughter's life, especially not before nationals," Mina bit back. The memory of Sunday afternoon still fresh in her mind. Lullu had taken her usual galivant on Boesman. She'd walked over to join her daughter to watch the sunset. That was when she'd seen him. Down on the beach. She'd heard he loved to run—that hadn't changed. But what caught her off guard was the plethora of emotions and sensations which invaded her body and heart when she'd looked down and seen Raymond standing there, looking at Lullu. He'd been topless in only shorts and trainers—his body as beautiful and strong as she remembered.

"Tell him he can see his Ray, but not to come near the house this time." Bile, fear, and pure stubbornness rode her words harder than a jockey racing his steed.

"You tell him yourself. Just like her father, she has a right to the truth. Besides, how's Derek going to be able to visit and not see Lullu? You know how close they are."

"Bloody hell, Ma! Derek cannot come to visit Lullu, and that's final." Mina exclaimed as she turned to find her daughter standing at the door of her study. Dark brown eyes gazed at her surreptitiously.

Shit!

"I've got to go. We'll talk about this in the morning." Mina ended the call and slowly placed her phone on her desk.

"It's rude to eavesdrop, lovie." Mina folded her arms across her chest.

"I wasn't. I got home from school and was looking for you, then heard you speaking of Oupa. Why can't he see me?"

Mina fell into her office chair and groaned as she wiped a hand down her face. It wasn't enough her abalone had been poached, or that she'd run in to Ray —now her daughter had caught wind of the one thing she was desperately trying to protect her from.

"Oupa can see you. You just heard parts of a conversation which has nothing to do with you." Mina relented.

"If it has nothing to do with me then why did you speak about me?" Lullu retorted, spun around, and stomped off.

Good Lord, when it rained it surely did pour. How was she going to navigate her family through this without scaring her daughter for life ... *or admitting that you're still in love with him?*

She fought back the last thought.

No, there couldn't be love left for Raymond—not after all these years and all that pain. She should hate him, despise him, find a way to get him off the program. Her heart thumped and her chest froze.

God damn this bloody asthma!

———

THE FOLLOWING Sunday Morning saw Mina, and Derek Le Roux watching Lullu train while her mom cooked lunch.

"Look, Oupa," Lullu called out as she performed a rear-ways up position on her pony.

The old man's eyes lit up. "That's my girl!" He threw Lullu a thumbs up.

"I don't know how your nerves hold it." He looked to Mina as she approached, shaking his head.

Mina waved a quick hello to Drina, Lullu's coach.

"Look Derek ...," now was the best time to broach the subject.

"Ray doesn't know, does he? How have you managed to keep all this from him?" The crisp blue of Derek's eyes softened as he placed a hand on her shoulder, glanced to Lullu, then returned his attention to her.

"I—erm ..."

"What, my dear?" The lines between his eyes deepened.

"He saw Lullu with me the other afternoon." She bit her bottom lip as she reached into her pocket for her inhaler. She'd been using it a lot more recently. No guesses as to why.

"And?"

"And nothing." Mina straightened then glanced to where her daughter was practicing before returning her hard gaze to rest on Derek.

"He wrote to me. He's been doing that a lot of late," Derek said.

"Shit. All communications are checked before being sent out." Mina shook her inhaler and brought it to her mouth.

"Easy now, my dear. He didn't put it in so many

words. If whoever checks the emails and letters has no idea there's a connection between the two of you, then believe me, they'd wouldn't have read what was stated between the lines," Derek soothed.

Mina closed her eyes and held her Ventolin-laden breath a moment longer before releasing it and giving her would-be father-in-law an angry glare. "Look, I don't want you discussing me around any of the others when you see Ray. Please, Derek."

The old man sighed. "You can't keep it from either of them forever, my dear; it'll only cause more pain. Besides, my son already has an inkling. Please don't hinder his recovery."

"Don't speak to me of pain, old man. I know I can't bubble wrap my daughter, but I swear, if it's within my power to prevent my child from getting hurt in any way, I will do so."

A look of regret flashed across Derek's face.

"Did you have a hand in all of this?" realization dawned on Mina.

Derek gave her a sheepish glance.

"Shit Derek!" Mina hissed at him.

"I'd do it again in a heart beat my dear." He stood a little straighter, his lips pulled tight and his eyes flashing with determination.

"Sorry," Mina whispered harshly as they both turned to watch Lullu dismount her horse using a rear-ways forward leap and tumble, "But you can't continue to complicate matters. And you'll certainly not tell him about Lullu!"

"It's not my story to tell. But if he asks, I will not lie to my son. I've kept this from him for too long."

Mina sighed and swallowed back her anxiety. "And if he fails rehabilitation, gets sent back to prison? What do I tell my daughter?"

"I don't think he'll fail this time. I truly believe Ray wants to atone and grow. Do better; be better." Derek's voice carried an assuredness a part of Mina desperately wanted to believe. "He wasn't always a rotten apple. I don't know what happened, but something broke him inside, the same something that is desperately trying to right his wrongs and step back in to the light."

"We'll see," she replied, scuffing her booted foot in the sand.

"Just know there is one thing both your ma and I have that neither of you do." Derek slid his arm around her and squeezed.

Mina had never known her father, and Derek Le Roux was the closest person to a paternal figure she'd had growing up. "And what is that?"

"Wisdom and the experience of life." Derek pulled her into a hug.

"So what ya think, hey Oupa? Boesman and I are so gonna nail nationals!" Lullu, Drina, and her horse strolled toward the pair.

"You're a wonder. An absolute marvel, my girl," Derek praised her from the fence. "I'll be back in a bit."

"Where are you going? Can I come too?" Lullu shouted after the old man.

"Not this time, *lossiepop*. Just going to see a friend." He winked and grinned.

"Is your friend that man who runs on the beach?" Lullu's words invited a cold silence to settle on Mina's heart.

Mina watched him make his way toward the far end of the garden and down the steps leading to the inmates' quarters when Lullu came to stand by her.

Derek's face remained blank and his nature calm, "Yes." He said then turned and walked off.

"Erm ... same time tomorrow. You're doing great." Drina smiled uncomfortably as she strolled by them, rucksack over her shoulder. "Lullu, you need to rub Boesman down and get him fed."

"Will do, Aunty Drina." Lullu smiled and waved.

"Are you cross with Oupa?" Lullu gave Mina a concerned glance as they walked Boesman to his stable.

"No." Mina shook her head.

"Well, something weird is going on with all of you."

Mina didn't reply. Best for the girl to assume than to continue asking questions Mina was unable—no, unwilling to answer.

"Come, your Omie is cooking us a wonderful lunch and is dying to hear all about your training." Mina cautiously diverted her daughter's mind from Derek and his visit.

———

"Won't Oupa be eating with us?" Lullu asked as she washed her hands at the basin.

Mina glanced at her mother, whose left eyebrow quirked. "He's having lunch with his friend; he'll join us for coffee and *koeksisters* later."

"But Omie's made much better food. I don't understand why I can't meet his friend too?" Lullu pulled out her chair.

Her daughters demands were trying her patience. "Lovie. Some things are best left alone. It's Oupa's private business. Now sit, please." Mina pointed to the chair and her daughter sat, but not before she gave Mina a knowing grin, which caused her insides to do a loop-the-loop.

Grace dished food onto their plates. Her yellow rice and fish curry was renowned back in Bo Kaap, where her mother lived.

"Mmmm, Omie, you always make the best curry." Lullu inhaled the warm delicate aroma.

Mina's tummy growled as the scents of chilli, fennel, and cumin found their way up her nose.

"Amen first," Grace commanded as Lullu lifted an overfull fork to her mouth.

Reaching out her work-worn hands to Mina and

Lullu, Grace began. "Dear Father in Heaven, we thank you for the blessing of this feast before us. We thank you for this beautiful day that we can spend together. Bless and hold our Lullu tight as she works hard for her next tournament—"

"And Boesman," Lullu interjected causing Mina to bite back a smile.

"Yes, and Boesman. Please bless that creature so that he may keep our angel safe," Grace added. "Thank you for this and everything. In your name, we pray ..."

"And also to keep Mommy's thoughts peaceful when she sleeps so her weird nightmares about my daddy can stop."

Mina's eyes shot open at the same moment as her mother's did. Lullu's remained tightly shut.

"Cheeky!" Mina mumbled.

"Yes, and please bring Mina some peace of mind and fill her heart with courage. Amen."

6

RAYMOND PACED THE FLOOR BESIDE THE TABLE AND TWO chairs reserved for him and Pa in the mess. All the other inmates' visitors had arrived and they were happily chatting and catching up.

To one side sat the counsellor, Vestra, and two guards strolled the outer edges of the hall. It struck Ray that there was no Mr. Meintjies pacing the floors and handing out scowls today. The man probably needed his time off too.

Excitement and panic roiled in his gut. Pa's letter had mentioned he'd visit today and that he was looking forward to it. But he was twenty minutes late. Had he changed his mind? Ray wouldn't be surprised. After all, it was his criminal actions which had landed his father on death's door.

"Ray." A deep, gravelly voice caused him to stop pacing and look up.

Pa, though older, hadn't changed. His hair was a little whiter, and there were a few extra lines around his mouth, but his eyes were as blue and loving as Ray always remembered them.

"Pa." He shoved his hands in to his pockets.

The old man wasted no time as he confidently strode toward Ray and wrapped him in a big bear hug. "It's so good to see the man I thought I'd lost." His father's words squeezed his heart.

Ray reciprocated the action, his strong arms curling around his father's portly form. "I missed you, Pa. I'm so sorr—"

His pa pulled away, still gripping Ray's shoulders in his strong, age-spotted hands. "You've already apologised. I accept. Now, let's sit down and catch up."

Ray swallowed the ocean of emotions threatening to bring him to tears. This was so like pa.

"Shall I get us some tea? The coffee's not what you'd like. Lunch will be served in a bit," Raymond offered.

"Sounds good, my boy."

Ray kept stealing glances at his father. It was surreal to see the old man, healthy and strong. He'd only seen him once after the attack which Ray was responsible for, and that had been at his sentencing months earlier. After everything he'd done to his family... who'd have thought he'd come to visit. It was a miracle. But what could he say to this man he owed so much to?

The pair sat at the table, cupping their mugs.

"How are you coping?" His pa folded his arms on the table top.

"I was doing fine until Mi ..." Ray paused when pa held up his hand.

"Shh, not now. We'll go for a walk after we've eaten." pa winked.

A bell chimed announcing visitors and inmates could make their way up to the serving area. Ray led his pa to the buffet. A spread put out to entertain their guests and one worthy of more sophistication than inmates entertaining family.

A tall scrawny man, with silver stubble and ratty strands of equally grey hair walked up behind where the pair stood in line awaiting their turn to dish up.

"This your pa?" Cyril held out a hand. "Pleased to meet you, *Oom*."

His pa gripped the man's hand. "And you."

"Have a *lekka* lunch." The man gripped his plate and walked off.

"Some colourful characters around here." Pa smiled when a second inmate proffered them a toothless smile.

"Ray's old man, huh?" the man asked, then leaning forward, saying, "This where you get the brains? He's the only one of us who understands the *larny* business of this farm." The inmate threw a thumb over his shoulder, indicating to Ray.

Ray shook his head as they returned to their tables with their food and cutlery.

"So, it seems you're doing well." Derek sat, then gripped his son's hand in his. "Shall we pray?"

Ray nodded and bowed his head as his father rambled his Afrikaans prayer of thanks off. The words were not new, but their meaning was refreshed. Ray quickly wiped away the single tear trekking down his cheek.

"I quite like the setup. It's the first time in a long while that I've found anything interesting," Ray said before shovelling a filled fork into his mouth.

Pa smiled broadly. "Good to hear, my boy. Good to hear."

They continued eating their bobotie and chatted about everyday stuff.

"Ja, these abalones, they're a pricey, sought-after food, but I never knew how important they were to the local ocean's ecosystem. I guess all the animals are," Ray continued to speak. He'd not felt so buoyant in years, and the fact that his pa was smiling and listening to him exceeded all his expectations for the day.

"She has quite the venture going here. I'm proud of you, son. You really seem to be taking your, er, issues in hand." Derek reached for the tin of soda he'd gotten with lunch, and sipped.

Ray averted his gaze and stared at the food on his plate.

"I won't let you down ever again, Pa." Ray reached forward and patted his old man's hand.

"I know. Oh, before I forget. I brought you a gift." Derek dug into his jacket pocket and pulled out a mid-sized square, brown paper-wrapped object.

"You shouldn't have." Ray hesitated when his pa handed it to him.

"Go on, my boy. Make an old man happy." Derek smiled.

Ray swallowed down his mouthful and took the gift. Fingers shaking and nerves tingling, he removed the tape holding the neatly folded sides.

From the wrapping Ray pulled a book bound in black leather. On its front cover, embossed in gold stood the title, *Blake the complete collection.* He lifted the book to his nose and inhaled, "I never could resist the smell of a good book."

No longer capable of swallowing his tears, Ray blinked and looked up. "Thank you." His hoarse appreciation came out as a whisper.

'Blake: the complete collection.'

"Thought you'd like it." Derek nodded proudly then continued to finish his plate of food. "Better to read than allow your thoughts to drift too much. You writing again?"

"On-only to you." Ray stumbled over his reply, wiping his eyes with the back of his hand, and placed the book on the table.

A soft silence wrapped around the pair. For the first

time in months, Ray felt something akin to the peace which had once filled his past and while it lasted, he allowed himself to revel in it.

"How's sis and Thomas?" He placed his knife and fork together on his half-eaten plate of food.

"Just back from a trip to Australia. She's working her arse off at that hospital, and Thomas is loving his new job with Interpol." Derek smiled.

"Do you think I can write to her yet? I owe them both a huge apology." Ray looked down at his plate.

"Yes. But I want you to listen to me first." Derek's voice grew deep and serious, forcing Ray to look his pa in the eye.

"I know you want to make amends, but it's not always their forgiveness that will enable you to move forward. Apologise if it's sincere, which I believe it is. I know they will accept it. Then, that is enough. Stop looking for atonement in others when it's only you who can give it to yourself. You cannot heal if you cannot forgive yourself."

Ray swallowed hard, clenching his hands together on his lap. Pa was right, but Pa had no idea how hard that simple request was.

"I've had to forgive myself for a lot too. I know it's not easy; it takes time, work, and love," Derek said as though reading Ray's mind.

"And what have you done that ever needed forgiveness?" Ray fought to keep the bitterness from his tone.

"Deserted my son in his time of need."

Ray's gaze focused on his father's face. The old man's bright blue gaze darkened, and the corners of his mouth turned down. "You and Ma were always there for me, Pa. It was me. I chose to ignore ..."

His pa quietened him with the wave of a hand. "I was too busy running the farm, hiding from your mother's diagnosis, and numbing myself to the pain of her loss. I forgot all about my children. I needed to forgive myself for not seeing what was right beneath my nose until it was too late. For a myriad of other times I failed you and your sister, not to mention Mina." He whispered her name.

Ray swallowed hard, "Did you know?"

Pa pinched his lips together, "Of the two of you? Ja."

"And you never said anything." Ray leaned away, not sure how to feel. Did he have a right to be angry?

"I figured you would... but then you ma and..." Pa's voice trailed off as he looked down.

"Grace has never left your employ. Did you keeps tabs on Mina? That girl..."

"Shhh. Not here. Come lets go walk down our lunch." Pa rose from the table.

The pair made their way over to the scullery, scraped their plates clean, and rinsed them before placing the dishes on the pile to be packed into the washer. Raymond tucked the book of poetry into his pants back pocket as he lead Pa outside, and they both walked up to the edge of the beach where the cement path ended and the hot sand began.

"You knew she owned this farm," Ray said.

"*Ja*. I called in a favour to have you sent here," his pa confessed, looking him right in the eye.

Ray shook his head and held up his hand. "Okay." It was all he could utter. The knowledge roiled in his gut.

"You are allowed to be upset with me." His pa acknowledged Ray's internal struggle.

"I am. But I also understand, or am trying to."

"Don't let that anger eat at you. You need to let it out, in a healthy way, and to know, this was the last tool in my kit. I'm your pa; how could I not always want to save you? It's not easy being a parent. Often there are no right or wrong decisions." His pa shoved his hands in his pant pockets.

His pa's words rung with truth, but Ray was still trying to make sense of the confession and his feelings. After years of burying them under a cloud of highs, it was hard to acknowledge and deal with them.

"Shall we walk?" Ray waved a hand toward the beach.

"*Ja*, but I'm taking off my shoes first."

Father and son laughed loudly as they hopped across the sun-baked sand like a pair of idiots. They reached the wet, cool part of the beach where the ocean's tongue lapped at the scorched sand.

"Eish. I didn't think it'd be that hot yet." Pa shook

his head as they both rolled up the legs of their trousers and walked.

Ray plucked up his courage and tackled the white elephant.

"I never meant to hurt her. I had to protect her. It didn't matter what it cost me; I couldn't let them harm her."

"I know, my boy. And not a day goes by that I don't blame myself also."

"How so?" Ray asked, confused.

"I should have protected you from those bigots. Don't you love how the idiots in this world believe only white men can be racist?"

Ray stopped as a wave crashed and sprinted up the sand, washing over their feet and up their calves.

Pa took off walking, leaving Ray to realize what his pa had just said.

"Do you think she'll ever forgive me?" Ray blurted as they rounded the far corner of the wide cove.

Pa bent over and picked up a sea-smoothed clam shell. He turned it this way and that, then looked at Ray. "That is a question you would need to ask her."

"She ran away the other day." Ray collected a few washed up pebbles and faced the ocean. Like him, it stirred and raged but also presented with moments of calm and translucent waves.

"It must have been a shock to you both after all these years?" Pa said.

Ray nodded, twisted his right arm and hip, then

threw a pebble as a wave crested before him. The stone skipped along the flattened water then dove in to an oncoming wave.

"Can't blame her. But the time will come when the both of you will need to face your pain and your past." Pa shrugged and turned back.

Ray enjoyed the sun and rush of froth and water in a shared silence as they made their way to the beach entrance. They rounded the last corner where the land peaked and formed a hill. The girl was back on the dune.

She shouted something and waved excitedly at them. Ray glanced at his father, whose face had taken on a stiff expression. Pa lifted his arm and returned the wave.

"Come, our time is almost up." He gripped Ray's elbow and urged them on.

"Is she mine?" Ray's eyes refused to leave the sublime real-life portrait of the girl and her horse. Even when his father's hand gripped his shoulder, he could not turn away from the scrawny blonde smiling down at them.

"You need to speak with Mina."

Ray's head snapped toward his pa. "But she's made it clear she wants nothing to do with me. Please, Pa. I have to know."

"And what peace will it bring you when you do?"

"It's better than wondering. Pa ... *is she mine?*" Ray pleaded.

His pa's grip tightened where it rested on his arm, "It's not for me to answer."

Ray's legs gave way and he plonked onto the sand. His world flipped then imploded. Pa didn't have to betray his confidences, Ray could see the answer plastered across the old man's face. He fell forward with his hands digging in to the hot sand. He needed an anchor. His blood screamed for a hit and his heart bashed itself against its cage.

Derek knelt beside him. "Now, more than ever, you will need your strength, my boy. You have a reason to become the man you once were."

"Why did you keep her from me?" He wasn't angry —only hurt.

"Why do you think? Your mother and I only found out just before she passed. She was just a baby, and you ..." His pa inhaled. The action was laden with painful memories. "... were lost to a world of darkness and drugs."

The old man rose with a groan and held out his hand to his son. "Come."

Ray reached up, gripped his father's hand, and stood.

"Now it's between you and Mina. Do you think you have it in you to be a dad, my boy?"

Ray returned his gaze to the hill. She was gone. "I don't know," he whispered.

He'd felt it that first time he'd seen her—a connection he couldn't quite explain.

"Well, I'm sure you'll get the opportunity to find out. You deserve it."

"Do I?" Ray pressed a fist into his diaphragm, which had spasmed in shock.

I have a daughter! I am a Pa!

But was he man enough, good enough to be allowed into her life? He had no right to ask that of Mina, not after what he'd done, even if every inch of his blackened soul yearned to be the man he'd promised her to be all those years ago.

"Life has a way of making even the worst situations work out for the best. You simply need to keep the faith, my boy." His pa's words rolled over him and watered the seed of hope he'd planted the day he'd run in to Mina.

Pa continued on their stroll and Ray followed. His head and his heart were spinning.

The pair walked up the path in silence as Ray led them to a tap so they could rinse their feet before putting on their shoes.

"It was good to see you. I think there is still much you must face, but this time you are not alone." Derek embraced him.

Ray waved as the old man made his way back up the steps toward the main house. He longed to follow his pa.

I have a daughter ...

Agh, who was he kidding? Father? He couldn't be a

parent to her. He'd given up that right the day he'd thrown Mina away like a soiled rag.

This was his place in the world now. A bottom feeder. A nobody who owed the world everything and deserved nothing. And yet his heart ached to reach out and be with them more than his lungs yearned for oxygen.

———

Mina looked up from her empty plate as Derek entered the kitchen.

"Oupa!" Lullu called as she strutted into the kitchen from the back door.

"Ah, back from your ride?" Derek asked.

"What? What ride? Lullu Marie van der Westhuizen, you said you were going to groom Boesman, not ride him," Mina scolded.

"Agh, Ma, he was antsy. He needed a bit of a run before he'd settle down. You know what men are like." Lullu brushed her mother's anger off and sat down at the table. "What's for pudding?"

Mina gave Derek a warning glance when he burst out laughing, and Grace shook her head as she rose and walked over to the fridge while Derek, trying hard to smother his humour, cleared the leftover cutlery and bowls from lunch. Mina simply leaned her head in her hands and sighed.

"Was that man your friend, Oupa?" Lullu asked as Derek took a seat across from her.

Mina's head shot up. She glared at Derek, who smiled and said, "Yup."

"He looks just like you from that photo of you and Ouma. You know, when you were also younger and thinner." Lullu giggled when Derek leaned forward to tickle her.

"It's all your Omie's good cooking." He patted his belly in an attempt to change the subject.

Mina felt her chest constrict. God! This girl was a bloodhound when she latched onto an idea, or in this case, the one thing Mina really didn't want her to discover.

"That's enough now, *bokkie*. Come, Omie has made your favourite pudding." Grace came to the rescue as she placed a plate of freshly made *koeksisters* and *melktert* before them.

"Ooo yummy!" Lullu said.

After they'd all finished the desert and coffee, milk for Lullu, and cleared the dishes, Derek stretched his arms up in to the air, "Ready Grace. It's a long drive back."

"Ja, it's time to go." Her mother smiled as she stroked Lullu, who'd snuggled in to her grandmother arms, head.

Mina walked her mother and Derek to the car. Lullu ran off to check on her pony, again.

"So, Ray wrote to me about the poachers." Derek's

voice took on the paternal tone he used whenever he got serious about things.

"*Ja*. But we're safe. They only wanted the abalone," Mina reassured him.

"Thank God. With all these farm attacks ..."

"You also live on a farm, Derek," she reminded him.

"True. We all need to stick together during these dark times."

"Look, I've got to ask ..." She paused and looked her pseudo father in the eye. "Do you think Ray ..." She swallowed when Derek frowned deeply. "Could he be involved?"

"No." His answer was swift and clear.

"With his past ..."

Derek held up a hand. "Six months ago, I'd have cornered him myself. But the man I saw today ... no, I can honestly say with a clear conscience that Raymond is not involved."

Mina nodded. She believed him. Derek had never beat around the bush when it came to his son's faults.

They continued on their walk to the car.

"You need to speak with him." Derek took her hand in his. "He knows, and I'll not play middle man any longer. "

Mina swallowed hard. "He doesn't deserve anything, Derek. I raised her. I'm the only parent she'll ever know."

"That's for your daughter to decide." Her mom spoke up.

"And what would you have done if my daddy had walked back into our lives?"

"Mina," Derek chastised.

"No, she's right, Derek." Grace leaned on her open door and smiled. "I'd have given you the choice, no matter how hard it was for me. But the difference is, you have proof he's changing. Your daddy never did come back, or change his ways."

Mina's shame at snapping at her mom burned inside her chest. Scoffing her feet in the dirt, she sighed. "She's thirteen, Ma. She's not old enough to make those sorts of decisions for herself."

Grace smiled, let go of the door, and walked up to her. She placed her hand on Mina's chest where her heart beat a stuttered thread. "Don't underestimate your daughter or the blood which flows through her veins, my girl."

"I know what he did was unforgiveable, but have you never wanted to know why?" Derek asked.

Mina wiped her hands down her face, "I asked him the week I found out I was pregnant. He told me to *vokoff* and said that I was a *kaffirs kind*. So do you still believe he deserves Lullu?" Mina had lowered her voice, but she made sure her tone sharpened her words.

Derek winced and shook his head. "Yes. He must have been very afraid for you if he'd used those words, as awful as what they are, my dear. A second chance is just that—unconditional. Didn't I once hear you say so?"

Mina's insides shook. She knew what Derek meant.

Tears stung her eyes, but she would not back down now. "That's different."

"Why? Because it's your heart on the line and not someone else's?" Derek cocked his head, a shadow darkening his gaze.

"No. Because it's my daughter—your granddaughter, Derek."

Smiling gently, he said, "Exactly. I'll be back for the next fortnight's visit." He slid behind the wheel.

Her mother hugged her, placing a gentle peck on her forehead. "You're not alone in this. Derek and I are always here for you." She climbed onto the passenger seat and closed the door, then gave her and Lullu, who came trotting up on horseback, a wave.

"Bye Oupa, bye Omie. I love you." Lullu waved back.

The car sped down the road away from the homestead.

Shit! Shit! Shit!

Mina reached into her pocket for her asthma pump. Why did she have to deal with Ray now? After all these years, when she had her life sorted out. Her business was flourishing. And the pieces of her heart were neatly tucked away for no one to touch.

Shaking the apparatus, she brought it to her mouth and inhaled, holding it, then slowly let it go. She was tired of all the stress and upheaval which had arrived with Ray.

"Come on. That's enough horsing around for today. I'm sure you have homework for tomorrow," she commanded Lullu, who rolled her eyes and lay flat with her back meeting the gelding's. "Fiiine," she drawled out.

Mina stomped back to the house, not wanting to see the inmate camp, when she stopped dead.

She'd had a number of small cottages built for her permanent workers. They sat prettily along the eastern corner she'd cleaned up beyond the back of the stables. There, she saw Ben and Becky. Their discussion looked serious. Agh. She didn't have it in her to mediate or even find out what it was about.

Turning her attention to her daughter, she waved for her to hurry up.

Mina made a mental note to ask Becky what the issue with Ben was. But all that'd have to wait.

She hated to admit it, but Derek and her mom had a point. She had to confront Ray.

7

MINA INHALED SHARPLY AS BEN STOOD, ARMS HANGING at his sides, looking down at his feet. Her morning had started off with a bang and a phone call from Abbe.

The desk was the only thing between Mina and Ben which kept her from grabbing him by the scruff of his neck and shaking sense in to his thick skull.

"What the fuck were you thinking?"

"I wasn't," he grumbled.

"Clearly. Ben, you of all people know how hard it is not to hand the locals a reason to give us grief, and then you, my manager, go out and pick a fight in one of their pubs." Mina stopped pacing and leaned with her balled fists on her study desk.

"To be fair, the *doos* was looking for *kak*, and he wasn't a local."

"So you *bliksemed* a holiday-maker!" Her voice rose an octave.

Seriously, she did not have the energy for this now. The poachers' trawler had been spotted a hundred nautical miles north of her farm, which for all intents and purposes posed a huge risk, and she still had to confront Raymond Le Roux.

She did not have time to manage her bad-tempered manager who'd set out on a path of self-destructive vigilantism, which had painted a bullseye on Redemption Farm. The papers were going to have a field day with this.

"*Vok*. No, Mina, I didn't simply walk into the bar and look for *ka*k. The man's known in the underworld for his links with poachers. I saw him pestering Becky earlier. The fact he's here in town, days after our break-in ... He's so hooked up, the cops won't even touch him." Ben placed both hands on his hips and straightened his back. His dark eyes were on fire.

"Great, so you picked a fight in town with the kind of crims the police don't even want to mess with. I need you here, not stoking the hatred of the people in Tatensrope, or attracting more attention from the poachers." Mina softened her tone as she sat.

"Sorry, boss. But I have a theory," he huffed.

Mina knew he was sincere. He only ever called her *boss* when he was making a point of showing her his respect. "Do you think Becky's involved?"

"Not sure. I spoke to her."

"I saw." Mina gave him a hard stare.

"Oh." He glanced down at his feet again.

"What did she have to say?"

"He was trolling for ass," Ben replied.

"Did you find anything out before you pummelled the poor bastard?" She waved for Ben to take a seat, but he refused. "Going to tell me who it was?"

Ben inhaled deeply as if to brace himself, sending a warning tremble down Mina's spine. "Jubejube."

"What the everlasting fuck!" Mina smacked both her flat hands on the table.

Jubejube was absolutely the kinda crim you did not mess around with. His rep preceded him—God, there was talk he had the province's premier in his pocket.

"I just lost it when I saw him here. I know he's involved."

"Is that your theory? Do you have proof?"

"I told Abbe before she locked me up for the afternoon." He wiped a hand over his freshly crew-cut head.

"And?"

"She said she'd look in to it. But boss, I'm telling you, be careful where you place your trust." He paced the width of her office.

"Gonna explain your theory any time soon Ben?" it irritated her that the man wasn't giving her a straight answer.

He stopped and leaned with both hands on the edge of her table, "This thing runs deep. There are big boys playing this game and they have too much to lose ..." He returned to pacing, stopped, turned to say something, but then decided not to.

"You need to tell me everything or I can't watch your back." Mina demanded.

"Obviously this is an inside job."

"Why?" Mina placed steepled hands beneath her chin. She wasn't convinced it was one of her people, if it were, the repercussions for her Redemption program would be far reaching.

"Common Boss. You'd need someone who knows the comings and goings of everyone. The way the system was tampered with...don't look at me like that Mina!"

"You do know your theory would include you as a suspect. Hell I fall under that umbrella too." Mina said.

Ben sighed and massaged his creased forehead with his hand, "Ja, I do, but I also know it's neither of us. I also don't think it's just one man feeding them info ..." He gripped the back of the chair Mina had offered him a few moments earlier. His lips pulled tight and his cheeks paled as his dark eyes stared out the window. "It's like a spider's web, but with more than one spider weaving it. I ..."

"What, Ben?" Mina was tired of half stories and fish hooks.

"Raymond Le Roux."

His words sent her insides cascading over the edge of the tight rope they'd balanced on.

"What of him?" She gritted her teeth.

"You know he was involved with those pieces of shit ..."

Mina stood, holding up her hand. "I've read his file. He had nothing to do with that."

"How sure are you? You know it only takes some cash, and his family is loaded."

"Enough. You have no place judging his family. As for him ..." She swallowed hard. "... he's not our man. Any other theories?"

"I'll tell you when I have something more solid." His phone buzzed and he abruptly pulled it from his breast pocket. "I've gotta go. Intombi Security are here to fix the mess down in warehouse five."

"About bloody time too." Mina huffed.

"Ja well that's Africa time for you." Ben slipped his phone back in his pocket.

"Okay ... just be careful please, Ben; you're not bulletproof. And if you're that worried about local enforcement, I think I may know someone who can help us out."

"Who?" His right eyebrow cocked sharply.

"A family friend." Mina nodded, rose from her seat, and mustered all her strength. It was now or never. " Before you see the security blokes, send Raymond Le Roux up, will you?"

Ben's expression shifted. A deep frown formed between his eyes. "I thought you said ..."

"Do it, Ben. And please, stay out of town for a bit,

and make sure these idiots replace the terminal with a foolproof system—if that even exists."

Ben nodded and stepped toward her. "It's not my place, but ..."

Mina didn't like where this was going. Ben had that look, the one he used when he got all soft for her. "Spit it out already."

"I know about Raymond Le Roux and your past ... about Lullu ..."

His words turned her blood to ice.

Holding up his hand, he said, "Your secret's safe with me, but ..."

Mina stepped out from behind her desk and straightened her back as far is it would go. It caused her pain to have to do this, but he was right. "You have no place, Ben Meintjies. Now, do as I asked, then go see to the security." Her tone crushed the warmth between them, confirming that at the end of the day, Mina was the boss and he was her employee.

Ben's shoulders stiffened as he nodded curtly, turned, and left.

———

"LE ROUX!" Mr. Meintjies voice barked across the warehouse to where Ray was shadowing one of the farm's employees as they tended to the baby abalone.

Ray looked to the worker, who said, "You better go. I can finish this."

"Okay." Ray turned and made his way to where Mr. Meintjies stood huffing and glaring up his nose at him. It was the only advantage Ray had over him, his height, and he secretly revelled in it. "The boss wants you up at the house."

Ray's insides flipped. He knew exactly who 'the boss' was that Ben referred to. Did this mean Mina was ready to speak to him, or had she found a way to get him kicked off the program? The last couple of days had been pure torture knowing what he now knew and not being able to do one damn thing about it.

He'd once again visited his regret, all the while battling the urge to simply give in. He'd found no answers except to keep his head down and carry on.

Vestra had been a godsend. He had to find a way to convince Mina to allow him to complete the program. He'd not cope if he was sent back to prison. While the rules here were stern and Mr. Meintjies was a bully, people were generally kinder. No, he couldn't let Mina send him back.

Anger and fear unfurled in his centre. He'd kept his distance and his mouth shut. He'd followed the program to the tee; he'd not fallen off the wagon like three of the inmates who'd arrived with him. And it wasn't as though the opportunities weren't ever present. He'd already been offered and declined some of the stash smuggled in.

He needed Redemption, with or without Mina. He needed it like he needed a hit.

"Don't waste her time. Get out of your overalls and move your fucking arse."

"Yes, sir," Ray replied.

He'd make her understand that sending him away now would be his end—he had to. He would promise not to go near their daughter; he'd promise his life if he had to. To stand any chance at all of ever being in his child's life, ever, he had to fix himself up for good.

"And Le Roux," Mr. Meintjies stopped him and leaned in until his nose almost touched Ray's. "Don't you put a fucking foot out of line or I'll have your balls for breakfast. I know you, and I know your type; I won't allow anything happen to her or Lullu." His sour breath washed over Ray, twisting his guts further as he digested the meaning sitting behind the man's words.

Nodding, Ray stepped away, turned and headed to the locker room.

Only the farm employees were in the warehouse when Ray walked briskly from the backroom where he'd left his gloves, overalls and gumboots. Mr. Meintjies had vanished, thank God. Now he understood why the man had gunned for him from day one. Was he that close to Mina that she'd confided who Ray was to her? That didn't matter now.

With knees that resembled jelly on a gravel road, Ray made his way through the inmate precinct and up the steps he'd watched his pa climb the day of his visit. At the summit, he turned back and looked down over the rooftops of the bungalows, mess hall, and ware-houses. The view of the ocean, which stretched until it trimmed the edges of the bright blue heavens, was right out of a fairy tale. His heart swelled and Ray took a moment to allow the wonder of nature to seep through his skin and fill the shattered hollow in his chest. No matter Mina's decision, he would not fail—not this time, and not ever again!

Clucking free-range chickens brought him back to the here and now, and the gauntlet placed before him. Bracing himself as he searched for a confidence he'd long ago lost, Ray made his way to the home's back door and knocked. It would have been inappropriate to assume the front door was meant for someone like him.

The kitchen was inviting and smelled of meaty humbleness. Paintings on the wall were from artists Ray had learned of in school, and the décor was comfortable with a modern twist, he noted as Becky, the woman who he assumed ran Mina's household, led him toward the far end of the house.

"Just wait here." The woman held up her hand as they approached a closed, beautiful lead-glass deco-rated door.

"*Ja,*" Mina's voice called.

The woman gently twisted the bronze door knob. "Inmate Le Roux is here, *mevrou,*" she said.

"Let him in. Thank you, Becky."

Ray sucked in a nervous breath when something on her arm caught his eye—a scar ... His focus was interrupted when she turned and said, "She will see you now." Her light brown gaze grazed over him coldly.

Ray nodded his thanks and entered the room. The back walls were lined with one long bookshelf adorned from ceiling to floor with colourful spines. To his left was a large window, and before him, his heart —Mina.

Dressed in a soft ivory-coloured blouse, with her hair tied into a neat bun at her neck, and her caramel skin flawless, she looked every bit 'the boss lady' of Redemption Farm.

"Take a seat, Ray." She waved toward one of two chairs tucked neatly into the front of her large white-washed desk.

"Look, I haven't done anything wrong. I've abided by the rules. I will—"

"Ray, please sit." Her curt command caused him to pause.

Ray nodded and did as he was told. Words of apology and justifications raced up his throat and filled his mouth, but Ray knew better.

"How are you?" He tried again.

Mina shifted in her leather seat and glanced at her computer screen, to him, and out the window, then finally, she settled a hard, dark gaze back on him. "I am fine."

Ray tried to hold her gaze but the longing in their

depths had him taking in every aspect of a face he'd missed more than he realised.

"Don't look at me like that." Her voice, hoarse but direct, accentuated her appeal as she folded her arms.

"Like what?" Ray asked sincerely, not realising what he'd done.

"Like you used to. You threw away that right a long time ago."

Ray's cheeks heated as he ducked his head and stared at his dusty work boots instead.

"We need to discuss ..." Her voice melted into nothing.

"Our daughter." He lifted his gaze.

Yes, he was a no-good crim who had utterly destroyed a young girl. But he was also a man who was willing to face his mistakes and fix what could be fixed ... and a father. This thought had struck him hardest a few nights before when he'd spent another hour doing sit-ups and push-ups to tame the demons.

"My daughter, Ray. Mine. You threw us away ..."

"I didn't know ..."

Mina jumped up from her seat and leaned across her desk, baring her white teeth at him as she gritted out, "And what difference would that have made, eh?"

Ray stood, dropping his arms beside him. "All the difference in the world."

"How so? All I was to you was a shag. A forbidden fruit you tossed the moment things got too heavy."

Years of shame, self-loathing and bitterness welled

in his gut, begging to explode in fury and justification. He could never go back to fix things, but he would be damned if he'd continue to be a coward also.

Tendrils of anger wrapped themselves around his neck and tightened, making it hard to breathe let alone speak as he balled his fists on his hips. "You're right. I threw you away like a cheap rag. What you don't know is that I had to!" He paused and allowed his confession to sink in. "I was young, stupid, and more than anything, I was so in love that yes, when things got heavy I didn't know who to turn to and did what I thought was best. I protected you. It cost me my soul, but I'd never had risked your safety because of others' hatred. As for *our* daughter ..." He waved a shaky index finger between them. "... if I'd known, I would have swallowed my fear and faced my pa. I would have sent those pieces of shit in my team to hell."

Ray plopped back into the chair. Confessions were exhausting and this one had cost him every ounce of energy he had.

Silence blanketed the room and Ray looked up to find Mina, face ashen, lips trembling, tears trickling from her eyes.

"You are not allowed to hurt me like this anymore. If I could, I'd have you removed from the program ..."

God she did want to boot him off, and there was nothing he could do to stop her, "Then why don't you, Mina? You owe me nothing. After all these years, you've done more with your life than you probably would have at my side. Kick me from the program. I am done." With effort, Ray stood once more and turned toward the door.

"I'd never take away your second chance, Ray. Like every other man who comes here, you deserve that much."

Ray didn't look back, couldn't.

"And does that second chance not include getting to know my daughter?"

Her gasp broke the broken pieces of his heart further.

He craved a hit more than the air he breathed. He was too weak to not love her and too stubborn to say so. Instead, he left her office and returned to work making sure he volunteered for the hardest, dirtiest labour there was to find.

———

MINA FELL into a weeping bundle on her chair. Curling her legs up beneath her bum and wrapping her arms around her knees, she buried her head and sobbed. She sobbed for the young Mina, whose life had been obliterated because of the hatred of others. She sobbed for all the years her daughter had lived without her father and she sobbed for the unconditional truth Ray had proffered.

God damn it all!

Damn fate, and damn her heart.

She'd never stopped loving him, and now, more than ever, she knew she never would. But to allow him back into her life, Lullu's life ... no, that would be a mistake—one she wasn't willing to make a second time.

8

"Ray, I do think you may be a little dramatic." Vestra, her dreads wrapped in a ball on top of her head, shifted in her chair, uncrossing her left leg and crossing her right. She lay her ebony gaze on Ray.

"How so?" He didn't mean to sound cocky, but did this woman have any idea what it felt like to claw oneself out of a dark shit-filled pit?

"Look I understand where you're coming from," she said knowingly.

"Now you're a mind reader?" Ray shifted uncomfortably.

Initially, he'd been grateful for the one-on-ones, but as time passed and Vestra dug her psychoanalytic nails into him, Ray was second guessing his decision.

Vestra sighed and placed her notepad and pen on the table beside her.

She uncrossed her long legs and leaned with her

elbows on her knees. "No, but I do recognise a soul who's trying to find the light. I didn't simply finish school and decide to become a counsellor, Ray. Life made sure I had my own little taste of its darker side before it showed me my way. It's not easy; you're right. But is anything that comes easily in life truly worth having?"

Ray digested her words as he turned his gaze toward the window. It was a shitty day outside. The wind could blow the hair off a dog's arse, and a storm was racing toward them off an angry ocean.

"Look, I'll be frank. I've known Mina for a long time. I know of both your pasts, together and apart. I also know that sooner rather than later, you will both have to sit down and face this past together. I want you to know, I'll be there for you."

Ray returned his gaze to Vestra and swallowed hard. "I don't think she wants to, and I don't blame her. Perhaps it would be easier if they transferred me."

It'd been a week since Mina had confirmed he was Lullu's father. It had only made things more compli-cated. Ray was finding it harder and harder to appease the turmoil threatening to wreak havoc in his mind.

"No, Ray. No transfer. Life has brought your paths back together for a reason. To ignore it would be to both your detriment ..." She paused and squinted. "... and your daughter's." Vestra reached forward and placed her beautifully manicured hand on his shoulder. "I can see you're struggling with your addiction. I won't have you backslide on my watch."

"I'm late for my shift." It was all Ray could say.

"Okay. But you know what to do if you feel yourself slipping. In the meantime, I will see to it that you and Mina get to sit down again, and this time I will be present. The longer you leave it, the worse it'll get."

Ray stood and nodded. "Thank you ... and sorry." He turned to leave the small consultation office.

"Sorry for what?"

Ray turned to face the woman. "There was a time in my life, one I am very ashamed of, but that needs to be acknowledged."

Vestra raised her eyebrows, steepling her hands beneath her chin. "You going to tell me?"

"You're a beautiful woman and a *blerrie* clever one too. I'm sorry I spent so many years allowing colour to influence my perception of the people in this world," he blurted, spun around, and walked out.

"Apology accepted," she called after him.

———

Ray rounded the hill and made for the far end of the bay. His running a saving grace. He pushed harder and faster. His body screamed for him to just give in to his craving, but his determination had other plans. He'd finished a hard day grafting in the warehouses, and still no word from Mina, but Pa had written, mentioning that Rochelle and Thomas were coming up. They wouldn't be there to see him, but to help Mina out with a problem. He was not to mention his brother-in-law's job with Interpol.

In the distance, Ray caught the shadow of a slim figure. The closer he came, the more it took shape. It was Mina's housekeeper, Becky, who stood staring out over the ocean.

Ray took a wide berth as he ran past her. A few hundred metres more, Ray turned and headed back.

Now the woman stood, smoking, her eyes on him as he came closer. She turned her head back toward the ocean and lifted her left hand to her mouth. Ray almost lost his footing when he noticed the mark on her arm. It had to have been her, the person he'd seen on the first night. She turned, her gaze fixed on him, her eyes bright with intrigue as a smirk spread across her face. Ray turned away. Shit.

The question was, who should he tell?

———

THE FOLLOWING AFTERNOON. Ray was summoned to the counsellor's office.

Vestra had not joked when she'd said she'd sit them both down.

Ray stood at the entrance to Vestra's office, looking to where the farm's counsellor sat opposite two chairs, one already taken by Mina.

"Hello Raymond. Please come in, sit down." Vestra waved to him as Mina's head snapped back, her eyes wide.

Ray didn't hide his surprise either. He'd really thought the woman was just trying to appease him. But here they were, barely a day after she'd made the promise.

"What the hell, Vessie?" Mina jumped up. Today she wore a dress. It suited her, all swaths of white cotton with a brown belt that matched the colour of the hair hanging loose around her shoulders. Ray had to force his gaze from her, afraid she'd catch him looking at her in that way again.

"Sit ,Mina. You know as well as I do that this needs to happen. For a counsellor who's always fought for her inmates to face their truths, you sure don't walk the talk."

"What's that supposed to mean?" Mina's voice took on a cold tone.

"That if you want your inmate to succeed, you need to be a part of his healing." Vestra smiled, her voice like a soft mist.

Ray closed the door and took his seat. The three of them sat in a semicircular formation with a small square table in the centre on which sat a box of tissues, two notepads with pens, and three bottles of water.

"I think we need to pin down the core of this problem." Vestra waved a finger between the pair.

"Why? Ray and I know perfectly well where this

started." Mina slapped her hands on her knees where she sat.

"And what of Lullu?" Vestra questioned softly.

"Same," Mina snapped.

Ray's reply made it to his mouth, but he bit it back when Vestra's glance told him to keep quiet.

"Perhaps a different approach is what we need." Vestra pointed with her gold Parker pen to the table. "Could each of you please grab a pen and notepad?"

"Vessie, I have shit to take care of and ..." Mina balked, but Vestra held up her hand and Mina's mouth snapped shut.

"That shit can wait, love. This shit ..." She gripped her pen, and with an index finger, made a swirling motion."... cannot. You need this about as much, if not more, than Raymond. I'm not suggesting you walk out of here holding hands, and dance off in to the sunset. But it's time you learned to deal."

"This won't fix the past." Mina pinched her hands beneath her arms.

"No, but it'll help to pave the way toward a better future. Isn't that why we're here?" Vestra's voice soothed.

"Fine." Mina threw her hands in the air.

In that moment she looked like the Mina of years past. Stubborn, scared, lost.

He so badly wanted to wrap his arms around her. Protect her. Instead Ray sat on his hands and bit his tongue.

"Right. Here's a writing pad and a pen for each of you. Write a letter to the other. It can be from your past self, or from your present self. Address it to the other."

"I've said what I have to." Mina sulked.

But Vestra ignored her, "It doesn't matter. Just write, don't hold back."

Half an hour and half a writing pad later, Ray handed his completed letter to Vestra, who declined it. "I told you to write it to Mina."

Ray retracted his arm and glanced at the pages folded neatly into an oblong.

Mina crumpled another page. "For fuck's sake!" She glared at Vestra then at Ray. "I'm done with this."

Vestra held both her hands up. "Okay. Don't give up just yet. Take Ray's letter. You have tonight and tomorrow to read, digest, and reply. We'll meet back in my office day after tomorrow where you can give it to him."

Raymond nodded and cautiously, as though he were handing a feral dog a piece of meat, and passed the letter to Mina who grabbed it, then shoved it in her pants pocket. "Fine. See you day after tomorrow."

She didn't give Ray a second glance as she stomped toward the door, slamming it behind her.

"Breathe, Ray. I think you've been holding your breath since you walked in. How do you feel?" Vestra offered him a bottle of water.

"I don't know," he whispered, looking at the closed door.

"She's a tough cookie, that one, but she's never had to face her demons or truly deal with all this shit. You left her; she was pregnant, and then she was a mother who had to cope with the condescending attitudes of a conservative community. A part of her will always be that frightened, heartbroken sixteen-year-old."

Ray nodded. "I wish ..."

"We all do. But don't get stuck there, my friend. This is all about moving forward. How are the cravings? Do you need extra help?" Vestra offered.

"I can handle them." Ray stood. "Thanks for this." He pointed to the writing pads before he walked out and into the humid spring breeze that drifted up off the ocean.

Was he handling this? Right then, Ray felt as though he were standing on a gangplank, staring down at a shark-infested ocean. Well, he'd have to deal with an irate Mina and his past if he wanted to play some part in Lullu's life.

———

THE STORM HIT SOON after dusk. A gale hammered its angry fists against the doors and windows of Mina's home. It'd drifted over them yesterday, only to return with more ferocity this evening.

"Do you think it will blow the roof off? It's made of straw mom, not tin like the warehouses." Lullu snuggled closer beneath her arm where they sat snug under the bedcovers in Mina's room.

"No. The guys who laid the thatch made sure it was meant for stormy Cape weather. We'll be okay."

"Ah, what if Boesman isn't? I need to go and fetch him, Mom. I'm sure he can fit in the kitchen." Lullu made to jump out of bed, but Mina squeezed her arm tighter around her daughter.

"Boesman is fine. His stables are made for this weather too, and you will mind never to try and fit that horse in my kitchen." Mina bit back her grin. *Ai*, this girl and her horse.

"But I don't think *he* knows that." Lullu tried to wriggle out from her mother's grip.

"He's survived many storms here, my love. Now, come lay down. I need to finish this work on my laptop, and you need to go to sleep. Tomorrow, you have your biology test and training. Nationals are around the corner." Mina tucked her daughter beneath the warm covers. The girl, almost as tall as her, curled into a ball and shut her eyes.

Mina leaned against the bedhead, not removing her gaze from the most amazing gift life had given her.

Memories of the day she was born rushed back.

"Push, mama," the midwife encouraged her.

"Come, bokkie. The baby's crowning; you're almost there." Her mom gripped her knee as she peered down to where the midwife positioned her hands over the crowning

head of the baby, gently escorting the small life in to the world.

"I can't ... arrrgh ..."

Spasms ripped across her belly and dug into her back. Her nether regions ached. She wanted to die, to scream, to curse the bastard who'd had the audacity to plant his seed in her belly! And then ...

"Agh here she is now," *the midwife called out as all the pain fled her limbs and her legs collapsed showing a blue, screaming, icky, white-smeared little ball of life in the woman's hands. She quickly wiped the screeching bundle down, and placed a bulbous instrument near the babies mouth and nose to suction any fluid or other ick which may be blocking her babies airways. Once satisfied, she laid the baby on Mina's chest.*

"A girl." Mina cooed as the tiniest rose budded lips smacked together at the scent of her breast. Ma reached down and guided the small head to her nipple and Lullu took to it without hesitation. The midwife smiled then busied herself with the umbilical cord.

"Ja. A beautiful daughter. Look at that. She's latched without issue."

It was love at first sight. A feeling so strong, stronger than what she'd felt for anyone else, flooded her entire being, and then she knew. Whatever she did in her life from here on out was for this precious bundle. Nothing was about her anymore.

She looked up to her mom. "I understand now."

It hadn't been easy, moving off the farm and into

the suburb of Bo Kaap. Nor had finishing high school as a single, teen mom in a community mostly made up of Muslims and Christian. The sleepless nights and early mornings had eaten at her soul. Thank God for Aunty Stiena, their next door neighbour, who had volunteered her time to watch baby Lullu while Mina went back to school.

Mina had survived all the finger-pointing and vile gossips. But it had made her strong. It had thickened her skin, which was just what she'd needed when going into business, opening a rehabilitation centre, and needing to stave off the pitchfork hungry uppity residents of Tatensrope.

Mina sighed. The Ray of her past deserved to know of their beautiful creature, but the Ray of now? Mina reached for the folded letter on her bedside table. It had burned a whole in her pant pockets.

Well, she supposed it was time to pull up her big girl undies and just get to it.

With trembling fingers, Mina unfolded the page. His handwriting was as beautiful as it had always been. She'd never met a person since who wrote so beautifully.

> *Raw grief, bitterness and mistrust,*
> *Shackled me to the past I lost*
> *It polluted my soul,*
> *Thought it'd leave us whole*
> *Facing years of wrongs,*
> *This fool, whose pride stood strong*

Deserves no gifts, no special treats,
No chance to reconcile or tell
My vain hope, eternal perhaps,
Might damn me to hell
But within fractured lines,
A story with no more lies
Wipe away the tears,
The shrapnel and the fears,
No sympathy do I seek,
Nor empathy, but only to speak.

Mina blinked several times to clear her vision. All she could do was stare at the pages. It'd been years since he'd written to her. She'd loved the words he'd strung out on paper when they'd been young. Wiping the back of her cotton three-quarter pyjama sleeve across her face, she straightened and continued to read.

I have to forgive myself for what I did to you. We were so young, so in love ... I still am.

Mina dropped her hands to her lap and swallowed. He still loved her ...

I'd rather be here now on my knees, my nose in the dirt, begging your forgiveness than visiting your grave, because, baby, that's where they would have put you if they'd had their way.

Mina dashed away the tears which blurred her vision as she read Ray's confession. She heard the voice of a young, scared boy between every comma and period. She saw the terror in a pair of blue eyes staring back at her that day in the storeroom when he'd called her that abominable name. Were these words enough to earn her forgiveness? She wasn't sure, but they were a start.

Mina closed her eyes. Still holding the letter in her hands, she leaned her head back.

A 'what if' slowly formed in the back of her mind. A vision of her and Ray on Nooitgedacht, the Le Roux wine farm. In her arms, their baby. On his face, unencumbered joy.

"I love you, baby." He cupped her cheek as he leaned over and placed a soft kiss on baby Lullu's head ...

9

A LOUD BANGING ON THE BACK DOOR WRENCHED MINA from her dreams.

Who in the seven fucks was that, and in a storm no less!

She'd nodded off where she sat, Ray's letter still in her hands.

Lullu was fast asleep, it seemed. Carefully, Mina slipped out from beneath the covers, placed the letter in the drawer of her bedside table, and grabbed her nightgown draped across the end of her bed. Not wasting time to slide her feet into her slippers, she trotted to the kitchen barefoot.

"What the *blerrie* hell ...?" She pulled open the door to find a drenched, pale, Klein Piet with a jacket pulled over his head for protection against the whipping rain.

"Miss. It's the roof of the mess and warehouse

three. The wind. Ma said I must let you know. Baas Ben has the men protecting the abalone babies and that you mustn't—"

"Get your arse inside. Go get a towel from the passage cupboard, then come sit down here in the kitchen and make a cup of coffee."

"Where you going, miss?" the boy asked.

"On second thought, go fetch Becky. I'll need her to watch Lullu."

Mina grabbed her polymer garden shoes and headed out toward her warehouses. The wind sprinted up off the ocean bringing with it sand and garden debris. Lightning lit up the sky and rain lashed at her face and soaked her clothes.

She'd be dammed if she lost any more stock. Not that she had control over the weather, but God and his angels should have known better than to threaten her livelihood.

Stumbling into the damaged warehouse, Mina wiped soaked tendrils of hair from her face and scanned the area.

"What the f—" Ben stomped toward her. "We have everything under control, Mina. You shouldn't be out in this." He placed his balled fists on his hips. Around him, inmates and employees scurried as they shifted and pulled protective tarps across the baths filled with baby sea snails.

"Don't think to tell me what to do, Ben Meintjies! How bad's the mess?"

His lips pulled tight as he heaved a sigh. "It's totalled. We'll need a new roof and to check all electrical equipment and sockets. Thank fuck you never tiled and left only concrete as flooring. Can you keep an eye? I need to go check the other warehouses for damage." Ben turned and headed out in to the angry night.

Mina nodded, then turned her attention to what was going on around her. Standing on the far side of the room, clad in only a T-shirt and shorts, hard at work saving her stock, stood Ray. Mina walked closer, forgetting about the chaos as she focused on the way his limbs moved and his muscles flexed. For a man who'd abused his body for more than a decade with drugs and alcohol, it looked as beautiful as it had when they were lovers.

Ray grabbed a nylon rope and tied it around a pylon, stretching a tarp over the pool. The rope unravelled, too slippery.

Without thinking, Mina walked up and grabbed the corner, pulling it down.

He glanced up, his eyes widening and his mouth opening then closing.

"Grab it." Mina motioned toward her hands pulling down hard on the rope. Ray nodded, then wound the rope tighter around his hand and pulled. He swung it around the pylon and began knotting it.

"Thanks." He nodded and made to move onto the

next job when a voice echoed out across the warehouse.

Mina turned; Becky was sprinting toward her.

"I tried to make her stay, I swear, but she kicked me in the shin." Her house manager lifted her trouser pants to show a blossoming bruise.

"Who? Lullu?" Mina called out.

"*Ja.* Boesman got out. She took off like a *springhaas*," Becky hissed and rubbed the wounded area on her lower leg.

Mina's legs buckled. *That bloody child, out in this storm.*

A strong hand grabbed her arm and kept her steady. Mina looked up and found Ray starring at Becky.

"Which direction?" His voice held a stern don't-fuck-with-me tone so unlike the injured dog who'd sat opposite her in Vestra's office.

"North, toward the nature reserve." Becky pointed behind her, an odd smirk flashing across her face before it turned to a frown.

Mina tugged free of his grip and made to go.

"I'm coming too." Ray followed her.

She was about to shut him down and put him in his place, but she couldn't do it alone. Ben was needed down here, and ...

"She's ours," he said simply, taking her hand in his. "We have no time to waste."

They made their way up to the house where Mina

pulled out three waterproof windbreakers, a towel, and a pair of torches from the scullery closet.

"We'll go in the *bakkie*." She pointed for them to retreat back into the storm.

———

TENSION BUNCHED IN HIS SHOULDERS. Nerves twisted his gut. Mina sped down the old path, the vehicle's lights on bright. Her chest began to ache and her breathing become painful. Damn it, she'd forgotten to grab her inhaler. Rain pelted the frantic wipers as they scoured the glass from left to right, unable to clear the windscreen.

"Could she have gotten this far away from home?" Ray asked as he bounced around in his seat.

"I'd hoped not. There might be one place they'd both head if Boesman ran too far from the stables."

Ray glanced at Mina, then back at the road ahead. He leaned forward and squinted. "Going to tell me?"

"The old farmhouse. It's in the direction she ran off."

It felt like an eternity before the *bakkie's* lights landed on dilapidated stone walls and a rusted tinned roof. Mina brought the car to a skidding halt and they both jumped out, torches shining brightly, rain beating down.

"Lullu!" they called out simultaneously.

Mina's head jerked toward him. Her eyes narrowed

before she turned and led him through a door-less entrance as she called again, "Lullu."

"Mommy!" came a strained cry.

Mina and Ray sprinted toward the far end of the old stone building. Ray's breath caught in his throat as his torchlight fell on a petite, shivering, drenched frame and a horse standing in the corner of the dilapidated farm house.

"*Blerrie* hell. I told you to stay put." Mina sped toward the girl, wrapped the large towel around her daughter, and rubbed down her body.

"Come. Let's go before this storm gets worse and the roof decides to fly off as well." Mina said.

"I'm not leaving Boesman!" Lullu pushed her mother away and wrapped her skinny arms around the gelding's neck

"Lullu Marie van der Westhuizen! For fuck's sake." Mina stomped her foot. The horse jumped and whinnied.

"Shh, boy. It's okay," Lullu calmed him.

Ray stood frozen. "You gave her ma's name?" He didn't mean to say it out loud.

Mina turned on him, and from the splintered bolts of light proffered by the angry colliding clouds above, he could see she was not impressed.

"Why'd you kick Becky?" Mina turned back to their daughter who had taken the towel she'd used to dry her a few moments earlier and was now wiping down the horse.

"I didn't even see Becky. I woke up, and you were gone, then I heard Boesman and ran to help him." Lullu raised her head indignantly.

A sharp bolt of light cut through the dark before a thundering blast reverberated across the earth. The horse whinnied and reared. The whites of his eyes grew larger than saucers. Ray's instinct was to pull the girls away, but Lullu barely flinched and reached out. The horse calmed and she wrapped her arms around his neck. "*Toe maar, Boesie*; it'll be okay. I won't leave you." She gave her mother a determined stare.

Ray snapped out of his shock. Clearly, the girl would not dessert her horse, and knowing Mina, she'd fight tooth and nail to get her way.

"Look. I reckon the old folks knew how to build. We're safer in here until the storm passes. I also think out in this weather, the horse might hurt himself. There's an old chair in the hallway I can break up for firewood. We can wait the worst of the weather out safely in here," he explained.

"I'm not sure." Mina sighed.

"We don't really have a choice." Ray nodded toward their daughter, staring suspiciously at him.

Lullu cocked her head at the same moment her mother placed balled fists on her hips.

"I saw you walking with Oupa the other day," Lullu said.

Mina glanced at her daughter, then Raymond, her lips pursing as her shoulders dropped. "You're prob-

ably right. I have a tarp behind the seat, and matches
and a candle in the cubby-hole."

"I'll get that. You clear out what you can from that
old fireplace. And you make sure to keep him calm."
Ray pointed a finger at the gelding before he turned
and headed out into the storm.

"Argh."

He spun around.

Mina, took a step forward, and buckled over
clutching her chest.

Ray ran to er side. "Geezus, are you okay?" Ray
wrapped his arms around her.

Lullu, left the horses side and knelt beside her
mother patting her pockets. "Mom, where's your
inhaler?"

"I ..." She wheezed. "... fo-got."

"You have asthma? Quick, Lullu. We need to get a
fire going."

He knew just what to do.

"One of my...er...cell mates," he glanced to Lullu,
"Suffered asthma. His inhaler was constantly stolen. So
he googled these breathing exercises to help hi whenever he had an attack and no asthma pump to help
him out."

———

WIND AND RAIN howled through the large broken
window at the far end of the room, but up where

they'd positioned themselves around the ancient fire-place, it couldn't quite reach them.

Ray sat with Mina's head on his lap and her back toward the fire for warmth. She coughed, inhaled, then coughed again.

"Inhale, hold...good now slowly let it go," Ray coached her through a breathing spasm.

"It's easing." She waved at Lullu.

Ray tucked a wayward strand of hair behind Mina's ear then poked the flames with the foot of the old chair. Lullu had found more fuel and soon their fire roared bright and warmed the large area, which Ray assumed must have once been the lounge.

He looked over to where Lullu now sat on the tarp, her horse beside her, his head on her lap. "You have a way with him."

Lullu looked up sleepily and smiled. "He's my soul mate."

Ray's eyes shot toward Mina. Their gazes met, and he knew she could read his soul.

"At least he won't break your heart." She pushed up from where she'd lain, then bit her lip as though she'd not meant to say that out aloud.

Ray fought the rush of emotions as the wind beat the old walls and battered the tinned roof. Was this what redemption was? An eternity of being reminded of one's past deeds no matter how hard you worked toward a better future?

Something in Ray flipped—whether it was a

switch, or just that he'd finally reached his fill of recrimination, he wasn't sure, but he'd had enough.

Standing with his shoulders straight and his hands clasped behind his back, he said, "You didn't read my letter."

"I did," she whispered harshly.

The shred of hope Ray had kept safe in his fractured heart flickered. He shook his head and sat back down, bringing his knees up to his chest, folding his arms around them. He should have simply kept his mouth shut.

"Too chicken shit to tell me back then?" Mina's voice was a whisper coated in acid.

"And you never told me of her."

Ray bit his tongue. He'd made his choice all those years ago. Arguing over his childish decision now wouldn't change anything.

"You goddamn coward!" Mina spat, then proceeded to cough and splutter. Ray stood and grabbed the empty tin he'd found in the *bakkie*. Holding it out the window, he collected some of the rainwater and brought it to her. "Drink." He held the tin to her mouth.

"Thanks." Her eyes reflected the flames. They glowed bronze and red as she peered over her shoulder to where her daughter now lay curled up beneath the towel beside her pony.

Lullu looked up sleepily and smiled, "He's my soul mate," she said, as her eyes fluttered closed.

"She asleep?" Ray nodded toward the sleeping beauty and her steed. His eyes hugged her bundled form. She was a part of him, no matter what anyone said. So perfect, so precious ...

"She'll never be a part of your life, Ray." Mina's voice, though softer, cut him like a jagged sword.

"I deserve your anger. But will you be able to forgive yourself when the sun comes out tomorrow?" He pointed a heated stare right at her. "I made a choice back then, a hard one, but one that saved you and our daughter, and it cost me everything. I'm no longer sorry that you can't grasp that fact."

She bit her lip. God she was driving him insane, emotionally and hormonally.

"Why? So that you can feel better about yourself?" She leaned forward on her knees and hands as though to challenge him.

Ray shook his head. "No, so that you can move on, and my child can have a father."

"You're a convict and a drug addict."

"One who's working his goddamned arse off to make up for a past I can never change." He focused on the flames dancing in the old stone hearth.

She sat back on her bum, her expression softening. "You're right. I'm sorry. But ... I don't know where to start. It's different with the inmates."

"You don't know them. They haven't hurt you. I have." Ray swallowed hard.

She was right; he was a coward, but he was also tired of running from it all.

Turning so that his body faced her and his back was to the fire, he crossed his legs and cupped his knees. "It was my fault. But I had to protect you."

"So you've said, half a dozen times."

Inhaling deeply, Ray closed his eyes and tried to centre his thoughts.

"Protect me from who, Raymond?"

"From Karl and his cronies, Benzile and Jantjie, Coach Stein, and the fucking rest of them," he shot back at her, then looked straight over to where Lullu still lay, asleep and exhaled.

Mina stood and paced the room, folding her arms around her. "I knew it was them." She stopped and glared down at him. "Why not tell me? We could have sorted it out together, gone to our parents ..." She stopped and drew in what sounded like a deep, painful breath.

"Calm down please. I'll get you back to the farm the moment the storm eases."

"Don't tell me what to do," she shifted closer to the fire.

Ray, so tired from the years of hiding from his pain, wiped both hands over his face. "Why didn't you tell me, Mina?" He pointed to their daughter.

Tears drowned her beautiful chocolate gaze. "Because of what you said."

Ray shuddered as the memory of calling her a *kaffirs kind* reverberated through his body.

He reached for her, but Mina pulled away. He dropped his arms at his side and they both stared at the flames devouring the pieces of wood they'd been fed. It didn't matter how hard he tried; she'd hate him forever.

"I shattered my own heart that day, sold my soul to the devil. I was afraid that if I told you, you would confront them. Mina, you have no idea what they would have done to you. They were a bunch of entitled, hate-filled bastards, and the only way I knew how to stop you from being hurt was to …"

"Break my heart too." Her voice trembled.

She closed the space between them. "Yes. It was the only thing I could think of to keep you safe. I should have gone to Pa, but he was old friends with Coach. I thought he'd turn me away too."

Ray turned to face her. A flash illuminated the room, and a sharp crack echoed out across the heavens. Mina jumped and Ray pulled her into him.

She was warm and fit so perfectly in his arms, the way she always had and he wished she always would. Mina didn't fight his embrace but gripped the collar of his jacket and leaned her head away. "Fuck you and thank you, Ray."

Tears streamed down her cheeks and over her plump mouth. Ray was drawn to her lips like the ocean to the shore. Leaning his head down, he gently touched her mouth with his. Her body tensed then relaxed, a soft sigh brushing his face. Ray only deepened his kiss when her hand brushed up the side of his neck, coming to rest on the back of his head. She pulled him in to her.

The years and the pain between them seemed to melt away as her sweet taste overrode both his senses and better knowing. Ray allowed his hands to glide up her back and cup her neck. His lips touched her cheeks and stroked her jaw, following the silky path down her neck ...

The couple jumped apart. The rustling of Lullu stirring reminding Ray they were not alone.

"Sorry," he apologised, suddenly afraid of what might or might not happen next.

"She's perfect." Mina twisted where she sat huddled on his lap, and looked from her daughter's sleeping form to him. "And so much like you it hurts to look at her on the hard days."

"The only good thing I ever did." His voice croaked.

"No. You have done many good things, but she surely is the most perfect. You're more than the sum of your past, Ray. You were bright, beautiful, and hungry to live life before ... and your sins are in the past. It's time to move forward."

"Is that the speech you give all the inmates?" He winced at his own words.

"Actually, it is. But they're true, and you need to hear them too. I saw the Ray I've always loved tonight.

You're in there, coming back to life. Don't give up ... please." Her plea almost broke his heart all over again.

"What now?" He had to know.

Mina shrugged. "Let's get through this storm first." She snuggled up to him, laying her head on his shoulder.

"That simple, eh?"

"No. I'm still pissed at you, and I'm still afraid of what you're capable of, but ..."

Ray shifted his head so he could see her face. "But?"

She bit her bottom lip, her eyes brimming with tears and fear. She sat up, cupped his face, and held his gaze with her own. "It scares the shit out of me, but I never stopped loving you.

10

Mina groaned. She'd confessed her love like a lovestruck teenager. *What the holy fuck?*

Ray said nothing. He only stroked her lips with his index finger. The sensation quickening her blood. His hand travelled across her cheek, and cupped her face. Leaning with his forehead against hers, the tips of their noses touched, "I love you too. I can be brave for both of us."

Convinced lightning had penetrated the tinned roof, striking her, Mina gave herself over to the electricity zinging through her body. She shifted forward and straddled Ray. His hands found their place beneath her shirt. The touch of his rough palms on her skin sent her heart galloping as she gripped the back of his head and kissed him so hard, she feared her lips might bleed.

The spot between her legs rubbed against his hard flesh. He groaned his pleasure into her mouth.

The damn horse whinnied, and they were once again reminded of their daughter laying asleep on the floor behind them.

"Uhm...," she cleared her throat, "We should probably..." she pointed with her thumb over her shoulder.

Ray grinned the same boyish grin from years ago. "Ja. Come, lie beside me. Tell me about our daughter." He slid down on the cold tarp, pulling her back into his front and stretching out an arm for her to rest her head on.

———

Mina woke with a start. A wet, sticky nose huffed in her face. "What the ...?"

Boesman's whinny was accompanied by a soft giggle.

"Eeeew! Boesman!" she chastised, and placed a flat hand on the side of the horse's face, pushing him away as she tried to sit up. Her body was cold and stiff from a night spent on the floor. Her arm wouldn't budge.

"You both smile when you sleep." Lullu came to stand beside her pony, grinning brightly down at her.

Mina turned to look through sleepy eyes to see why her left arm wouldn't budge and gasped as she found it tucked neatly beneath Ray in the early dawn light.

Shit!

With force, she ripped it away, and Ray jumped up, alert and on the defensive.

Lullu's horse whinnied and shook his head.

"Shh, Boesie. It's okay," Lullu calmed him.

Mina leaned forward, placing her elbows on her knees and her face in her hands. How was she going to explain this to her daughter, and what the everlasting heck had gotten into her last night?

"We better get back ... dammit!" She stood and searched her jacket and pants pockets.

"What?" Ray brushed his hands through his hair, avoiding eye contact with both his daughter and her.

"I left my phone at home. Ben's probably got the entire police force out hunting for us."

"Don't worry, Mom. Boesman and I will ride ahead. I'll explain everything to Oom Ben and tell him you and my daddy are on your way in the *bakkie*." Lullu stepped forward and gripped Ray's hand in hers. A tsunami of emotions threatened to overwhelm Mina. Looking to Ray, his sapphire blue eyes rimmed with tears. He bit his quivering lip as his Adam's apple bobbed up and down in his neck.

"I look forward to getting to know you." Lullu smiled, returned to her pony, and flung an arm around his neck.

Mina Stood frozen to the spot. Ray didn't move either as Lullu flipped herself onto the horses bare back.

The pair were out of the room and shot through

the front entrance, galloping across the sands before either Mina or Ray were able to understand what had just happened.

"When did you tell her?" Ray asked.

"I didn't." Mina wiped her hands over her face trying to digest what had just happened.

"Very intuitive for a thirteen-year-old," Ray mumbled, more to himself than Mina.

"Welcome to my world." She shook her head as she grabbed the tarp from the floor.

———

MINA CLUNG to the vehicle's steering wheel as she allowed the gravity of last night and the morning's happenings to sink in. Her knuckles blanched, and her jaw ached from gritting her teeth.

"Did she figure us out on her own?" Ray's voice was rough and thick with emotion.

"Must have. She's not like other teens her age."

"Clearly," he replied, looking out the passenger window.

Mina pressed down hard on the petrol pedal and the *bakkie* sped across the old, rarely used dirt road. There would be a world of shit waiting for her at the farm house.

"Look. I don't care what was said last night. It doesn't change how I feel. When we get back, you need to return to your cabin and your duties. It's important you complete the program; it's the law."

"And then, Mina? Where do we go from here? What will happen once I've completed the program? Don't get me wrong. I want to move forward. But with both of you in my life, and I'm not sure how to do that."

Mina slammed the dash. "Goddammit, Ray. You've brought nothing but chaos back into my life. Just give me today to fucking sort out the world of *kak* we're returning to, okay? Can you do that one thing for me?"

Ray pushed back into his seat and the pair sat in silence for a moment.

"Sorry I didn't mean to lose my shit like that. I'm just feeling a little overwhelmed."

"You and me both," he replied as they drove over the last mound and the farmhouse came in to view.

"Agh, my *goedigge vok!*" Mina took in the chaos stationed around the back of her home.

Cars and flashing lights stood parked around the back of the house and stables. Mina could make out Lullu and Boesman. Ben was standing beside the horse, and Abbe and a constable were chatting to couple she recognised immediately, and by the way Ray shifted in his seat beside her, he did too.

"Your sister and Thomas are here." Mina sighed as she pulled up to the circus awaiting them.

She brought the *bakkie* to a skidding halt and sucked in her breath as both Abbe and her constable aimed their weapons at Ray.

"Put your hands where I can see them, Inmate Le Roux," Abbe commanded.

"Put that away!" Mina yelled out her open window to Abbe and her colleague. Ray remained sitting in the passenger seat, hands raised in surrender.

"He's been with me, and we are fine. He had permission to leave the inmate area last night."

"That's what I told them Mom. But no ... I'm a kid. Who believes me?" Lullu waved her hands in the air.

Abbe cocked her head as Ben stormed toward them.

"Ben! Calm down, now." Mina ordered and the burly man skidded to a halt, huffing and fixing his fuming gaze on Ray.

"Everything's okay. Lullu ran off after Boesman last night. We followed and found shelter in the old farm-house. Now, Abbe, I am sure you and your constable have better things to do." Then, she turned to Ben. "Leave him be."

Abbe and her constable replaced their weapons. "If you're sure."

"I am. Thanks." Mina waved.

Ray slowly alighted from the car as his sister, Rochelle, and her husband, Thomas, walked up to them.

"Well you really didn't have to summon the cavalry for our arrival." His brother in law joked.

"See you two have reconnected." Rochelle nodded toward Ray then embraced Mina, "It's been a while."

Mina gave the woman a quick hug then stepped back. "Sure has. Thanks for coming."

Ray stepped forward holding out his hand, "Hello Sis, Thomas. It's good to have here."

Rochelle stepped back, her gaze guarded and cold, but her husband took Ray's hand and shook it. "Good to see you, Raymond."

"You need to get back to the camp, please." Mina said.

"On my way." He proffered a shy smile.

"You okay?" Rochelle placed her hands on Mina's shoulders, "you're wheezing."

"Okay," holding out a hand, "Hello sis, Thomas. It's good to have you here."

———

RAY ZOMBIE-WALKED BACK to his cabin. He wasn't sure what he felt, but the understanding that he had something more important than himself to fight for raged against his current situation.

He was a father to a girl with the spirit of a wild mare. Not only that, the woman he'd always loved and would always love still loved him too.

Where to from there? He had no idea except that he would work his soul and his fingers to the bone to be the best he could for them both. He'd never lose them again, ever.

"Le Roux!" the familiar voice rumbled across the air like a stampeding bull elephant.

Ray turned and came nose-to-nose with an angry Ben Meintjies.

"Who the fuck do you think you are?" Ben grabbed him by his shirt.

Ray's instinct took hold. He slapped both his flat hands against the man's chest. Ben, caught off-guard, stumbled backward, skidded, and, like a bull aiming for a red muleta, raced at Ray.

"You think you're the bee's fucking knees." Spittle splattered across Ray's cheeks as Ben grabbed him once again by the collar.

Sensibility settled Ray's temper, and he bit back his retaliation. Ben was big, but bullies were always driven by their anger; he'd easily take him down except that the last thing Mina needed was him getting into a fight with her manager.

"I have work to get to, sir." Ray gritted his teeth, took hold of Ben's hand, and forced him to let go as he stepped away.

"Work? You think you still have a place left here after the shit you just pulled?" Ben yelled. "Pack your bags. You're done." Ben pointed in the direction of the farm's gate.

"I'm done when the boss says I'm done," Ray replied and tried to walk past Ben, who placed his hand on Ray's chest.

"Are you stupid or deaf? I said you're outta here.

This is my farm and those two"—he pointed toward the farmhouse—"are my responsibility. And I believe you're the reason this farm was targeted. I'll protect them, which is more than I can say for you."

Ray's temper rose. He clenched a fist he badly wanted to land squarely in the man's face. "Just let me get back to work, sir."

Ben's grip tightened around the fabric of Ray's T-shirt. "Pack your *blerrie* things. You have no place here or in their lives. Lullu doesn't need a piece of shit like you as a father."

Ray's head snapped to the side. He met Ben's dark stare with one of his own. "It's not your decision to make, nor is it any of your business." God, he wanted to—no, needed to put this asshole down, but that could cost him dearly, and he wasn't about to lose everything he'd fought so hard to regain.

Ben pulled back with his free arm. His large hurtled toward Ray's jaw. Ray ducked, swung right, and retaliated with sharp jab to the man's sternum effectively knocking the wind from his sails. This was the one of the few good moves he'd learned over the years drifting in and out of prison—how to fight and fight dirty.

"Enough!" a voice whipped across him as Thomas and Mina hurried toward them.

"Ray, get cleaned up and go to work. Ben, to my office, now," she instructed, helping Ben up from where he'd fallen flat on his backside, heaving and spluttering.

Ray felt the smallest sliver of envy as Mina slid her arm beneath the burly bully's and helped him to stand.

"You okay?" Thomas's genuine concern caught Ray off-guard. He waved the man away.

"Yeah." Ray nodded and returned to his cabin where he grabbed his toiletries and work uniform.

He'd have to watch his back from here on out. With Ben gunning for him, he wasn't safe.

———

HOT WATER SOAKED the flesh of his stiff body.

While every one of his dreams had come true last night, the tarp had not made the cold concrete farmhouse floor any more comfortable to sleep on. The shower relieved some of the stiffness, but his back and neck still complained as he moved.

Ray grabbed his washcloth and cake of soap, then rubbed the two together before washing his body. Memories of how good she'd tasted and how she'd enjoyed riding his hard-on before they'd been reminded of Lullu asleep in the corner aroused him.

Looking over his shoulder to make sure he was alone in the cloakroom, Ray took himself in hand.

He imagined Mina naked and riding him, her breasts bouncing and her nipples puckered. In his mind's eye, he felt the hard buds of her nipples as he rolled them between his thumb and index finger. Her wet hunger pushed down on him as she begged for more with lips as plump as ripe strawberries. His fist worked harder as the images he played across his mind intensified. Relief flooded his muscles and his climax washed down the drain with the water.

Ray leaned with both hands against the wall, a little ashamed of his actions, but frighteningly content.

11

"So, Pa said he'd told you why we're here." Thomas accompanied Ray to one of the warehouses. He'd found his brother-in-law waiting for him outside his cabin when he'd returned from his shower.

"Ja," Ray replied.

He wasn't sure what to do or say to Thomas. Last time he'd seen him, Ray had been as high as a kite, in his pa's kitchen, and this man had been about to give him a solid hiding for disrespecting Rochelle.

"Hey." Thomas stopped. "Look, I understand you're uncomfortable. But honestly, if you can see a way, perhaps we could leave the past where it belongs."

Ray looked at his feet then out across an ocean which bore the brunt of last night's storm. Its waters were murky and laden with debris.

"How? What I did ... what I said ..." He faced the man.

"It's behind us." Thomas tucked his hands in to his pockets.

"How do you do it?" Ray kept his gaze on Thomas's face.

"What?"

"Forgive so easily, or are you taking the piss?" Ray wasn't sure any man could simply let go of shit the way Thomas seemed to be doing.

"It's not easy, and I can do it because more than anything, your pa wants his family whole again. If Pa believes in you, so do I." Thomas smiled sincerely.

"And Shelley?"

"You know she hates you calling her that," Thomas chastised lightly.

"Sorry. But what about her? She still hates me. Can't blame her though." Ray kicked with his boot against the paved walkway.

"You're her brother. She doesn't hate you, but it might take you a while longer to earn back her trust."

"Fair enough." Ray shrugged. "Look, I'm already late. Is there anything you need from me or can I get to work?"

"I'll walk with you. Pretend I am someone you're showing around. In the meantime, have you seen anything out of place?" Thomas waved in the direction they were heading before they stopped.

Ray took a deep breath, and slid the happenings of the last twenty-four hours and his impending showdown with Ben to the back of his mind. "Man, now you mention it ..." Ray made sure no one was in earshot as he told Thomas of the first night he'd arrived and seen the torch signalling. He told him about the scar and that he thought that perhaps Becky, the housemaid, had a similar marking on her arm, but that he wasn't entirely sure.

———

"Thanks for this." Mina showed Rochelle to the guest room where she and Thomas would spend the next few nights.

"No sweat, sister." Rochelle smiled as she placed their suitcase against the wall and plonked down of the large king-sized bed, patting the area beside her. "You want to tell me what Ray and you got up to last night?"

"Wh—me and—erm ..." Heat exploded across her cheeks as she stuttered and looked everywhere except at the woman grinning back at her.

"Sit." Rochelle patted the bed again.

Mina obeyed.

"It was painted across both your faces, not to mention Lullu blurting it out to the world that she'd found her dad, and you were bringing him home."

"Arrg. That daughter of mine ..." Mina groaned slapping her hands to her forehead.

"Is every bit of what you'd get if you and Ray were

put in a pot and stirred." Rochelle laughed, and Mina couldn't help but join in.

"You'll just have to settle things with Ben though," Rochelle added, dampening their laughter.

"What do you mean?" Mina bit her lip. If it was that obvious to an outsider, maybe her Ben problem was bigger than she thought.

"He's always had his sights set on you." Rochelle bumped her shoulder against Mina's.

"Ja. I've had to put him in his place." Shook her head then stilled a moment, "You don't seem too upset about seeing Ray." Mina changed the subject.

Rochelle exhaled hard. "Don't get me wrong—I still owe him a decent *what for*, and it'll take me a long time to forget what he did to Pa, but ... and I don't say this lightly ... the look on Pa's face when he got home last Sunday, and the utter joy bubbling from your girl this morning? It's enough to give me some hope of him ..." She pursed her lips. "... improving. And you two seem to have moved on?"

"Yes and no. We have a long ways to go. But now I have some poachers to catch first. I can't afford another break-in and I still have no clue who the inside man could possibly be." Mina stood. "I need a shower and some breakfast. Meet me in the kitchen. I think I might just put you to work too while you're here. There're a couple of inmates and my employees who could do with a good doctor, if that's okay with you?" Mina hoped she hadn't overstepped. She and Rochelle had always got on well but things were so over the top at the moment, she wasn't sure where to grip or where to let go.

"Of course! I brought along my bag and supplies. Had a feeling they might come in handy."

———————

ALONE AT LAST!

Mina hugged her coffee mug as she leaned back in her study chair and gazed out the window. Boesman stood grazing from his trough as though he'd caused not a drop of trouble the night before. The sky reflected a brilliant blue with all remaining storm clouds gone.

She needed some space to deal with the hoard of rampaging emotions creating havoc in her heart and mind. What happened last night between her and Ray both excited and scared the living daylights out of her. She'd come so close to giving all of herself to him again, to breaking her promise to herself, but her body had exploded with memories and hunger. Thank God Lullu had been there, asleep, but present. But had Mina allowed herself to hope when there was none?

There'd been no further exchange between her and Lullu about last night, or the fact that Ray was her father. Mina wasn't sure if this was a good thing or potentially a bomb waiting to go off in her face.

She decided to keep Lullu home from school after

the night they'd had. But instead of resting up, her daughter had quickly glued herself to her aunty's side and followed her to the camp. There was no point in keeping her away now.

A soft knock on her door drew her away from her pondering. "Yup?"

Thomas stepped inside. "Hey. You got a minute?"

"Sure. You found something?" She waved for him to take a seat.

Thomas closed the door and sat. "I have suspicions, but nothing solid, sorry."

"Ugh, you sound like Ben." She wiped a hand down her face.

"Ben?" Thomas cocked his head.

"He's been doing his own investigation on the side. Even got into a bar fight with some so-called gang member seen in town ... anyway." She crossed her legs and unfolded her arms. "I spoke to Abbe and the guy's gone and no charges were laid, thank God."

"Did he mention who the bloke was?" Thomas stroked his chin with a thumb and index finger.

Mina hesitated. "Jubejube."

Thomas's lips pulled tight and his nostrils flared. "Hmm, not sure if that was a wise move on his part." Thomas pulled a small notepad from his pocket and scribbled something in to it.

"You obviously know of him."

"Yeah. A nasty piece of work, wiley, too. Never

leaves enough evidence for anyone to make an arrest," Thomas replied.

"Well, you going to tell me what your angle is?" Mina placed her mug on the table. "Want one, by the way?"

"Nah, all good, thanks. I don't have an angle. It's pretty straight forward except that I need to find the evidence and accomplices." He placed the notebook and pen on her desk. "Tell me about your employees. Start with Ben, then with Becky and her son."

Mina straightened her back. "Ben's a good man—how many times do I have to tell everyone? And why do you suspect my house manager?" Mina paused.

"What?" Thomas asked.

"Last night in the storm, Becky'd accused Lullu of kicking her. But Lullu swore she'd not seen her at all before going after Boesman." Mina said.

"It could be nothing. I'm sure everyone was stressed, or..." Thomas tapped an index finger on his chin.

"Or? Why would she lie about it? I saw the bruise." Mina shook her head, "It's probably nothing."

Thomas sighed. "I don't like to jump to conclusions. But this is a serious investigation; it's a process. Speculation and fact finding."

Mina glanced out her window, then returned her attention to Thomas.

"Okay. So is she a suspect?" Mina asked.

Thomas's shoulders rose and fell as he clasped his hands. "When I accompanied my niece to feed her horse this morning, neither of us could find any evidence of him having kicked the stable door out. The latch was still intact. Is the horse able to open it by himself?"

"With that gelding, anything's possible. I don't know who would have let him out or why?" Mina found Thomas's observation worrying. Perhaps Lullu had been so fraught she'd not remembered Becky being in the house...

"Klein Piet was also supposed to be here."

"Where? In the house?" Thomas picked up his pen.

"Yes. I told him not to go anywhere while I went down to check out the damage."

"Hmmm." Thomas scribbled in his notebook.

"Are you going to question them? I'd hate for us to be wrong. People take offense really easily these days." Mina said.

"It's a good place to start. She is one, and possibly this Klein Piet."

"He's her son." Mina said. "But in all truth, I can't see either of them being diabolical enough to pull something like that off."

"Then there's Ben, who works closely at your side and knows your coming and goings. Your manager has a past. He's kept his nose clean these last years, but ... it's logical. Also, have the police given you their report on their findings yet?"

Mina nodded. "Makes sense. And yes. I printed it and ..." Mina slid open her drawer where she'd placed the folder containing the police report, security company's findings, and notes Ben had taken of eye-witness reports.

She rummaged beneath the other manila folders.

"What the ...?" Mina bounced up off her chair and opened a cabinet of drawers behind her.

"Something the matter?" Thomas rose from his seat.

"*Ja*. I'm very organised when it comes to my admin. I know for a fact I left the folder ... aah, what's it doing in here?" Mina pulled the folder out from the back of the second drawer.

"Could you have shoved it behind all the others files if you were in a rush?" Thomas walked around to where Mina was.

"I would never do that." She turned and placed the crumpled folder on her desk. "Someone's been in here."

"There are the obvious suspects," Thomas added as he flipped open the file.

"Shit! The report, Ben's notes ... they're gone. I did leave Klein Piet and Becky to look after Lullu last night. But I'm sure the house was left open and empty when Lullu ran off, so anyone could have come in."

"Deep breath, Mina." Thomas patted her back. "Sit down." He waved to her chair then walked over to the study door, placed his ear against it, then opened it abruptly.

Mina eyes widened. "What the hell?"

"Making sure we're alone." Thomas gently closed it and returned to his seat. "Now, what do you know about Becky's son, Klein Piet?"

12

RAY SPRINTED THE LAST FIFTY METRES AS HE NEARED THE end of the bay, slowed, and turned. It'd been a difficult and long day. He resolved to find time tomorrow to ask Mina if they, Lullu included, could have a sit-down session with Vestra.

Their situation needed resolving and a decision made as to what the future held for all of them. Mina had quickly raised her wall this morning when they'd arrived back at the farmhouse, and he was no longer sure where he stood with her. Yes, she'd confessed she still loved him, and he'd never stopped loving her, but after all was said and done, was that all they needed to let go of the past?

News of what had happened spread amongst the workers and inmates like wildfire, and everyone had walked a wide berth around him the entire day—everyone, that was, except for Ben, who'd gone out of his way to give Ray the shittiest jobs and chided him every chance he got.

But this wasn't his first rodeo. He could deal.

What ate at him was the way the bloke had looked at Mina this morning when she and Thomas had intervened. He was in love with her. Not only was that a problem, but it had stirred the long-sleeping green monster within Ray.

Was Mina involved with Ben? Was that the reason for her distancing herself? These were the questions he needed answers to so that he could move forward.

A thick mist began to blow in off the ocean. Just beyond the next dune, Ray could make out a slight form. He picked up his pace, the mist cleared. Mina was strolling up the strand, her head bent forward, kicking her feet in the sand. She not yet seen him.

He slowed as he neared her. Mina stopped and looked up. What Ray saw staring back at him, nailed him to a proverbial cross.

"What's wrong?" He trotted up to her, not thinking of anything but his need to chase away the thing hurting her. He cupped her face and searched her red-rimmed eyes for answers.

Mina fell into him and began to weep. Tears soaked his skin and the sensation of her breasts pushing against his chest sent ripples of heat coursing through his veins.

Ray sat them down on the sand and cradled her in his arms. He remained silent, allowing her to exorcise her emotions. The world turned, and the breeze continued to drift off the roaring ocean, and still, Ray cradled the only woman he'd ever love.

After a while, Mina sniffed and pushed up from where she had lain against Ray's chest. Using the hem of her dress, she wiped her face, giving Ray a glimpse of her inner thigh.

Ray forced himself to look away.

"I'm sorry." She sniffed.

"What happened?" he asked, tucking a wayward chocolate strand behind her ear.

"Everything,." She waved her hands in the air. "You! The fucking poachers, Ben Meintjies," she blurted between sniffs and hiccups.

The mention of Ben's name drove a spike deep into Ray's soul.

"I'm sorry." Ray wasn't sure if that was what she needed, but he meant it.

"Fuck you, Ray. Sorry doesn't even begin to fix it." She slapped his arm.

"I deserve that."

Mina looked him in the eye, her gaze soft and warm. She wrapped her arms around his neck and began to sob again. "It must have been so hard for you. I'm sorry I didn't try harder ... Should have told you ... I should have..."

Years of raw emotions burned their way up Ray's throat and bulged in his neck.

He swallowed hard, and his voice broke when he

replied, "Should-haves and could-haves are irrelevant. We are here now. Life brought us back together for whatever reason. We have this amazing daughter you raised on your own. You have a life that's better than any I could have provided ..."

"Oh, bullshit!" Mina leaned back, her eyes puffy but angry. "It should have been a life with you! That was all I ever wanted, Ray. Why are women forced to believe that they have to make it on their own? Be tough, be trendsetters, make no room for a decent partner to love and be loved by or they're failures, weak, and oppressed. With you, I was everything I wanted to be. I love that there are strong female figures out there for my daughter to look up to, but I just wanted to be yours!" Her hands gripped his shoulders and shook.

All coherent words and thoughts fled Ray's mind in that moment. Surely this was a dream. He pinched himself. "*Eina!*"

"What did you go and do that for?" Mina laughed. God, what a sound. Deep-bellied and joy-filled—how much he'd missed her.

"Thought I might be having one of those dreams again." He shifted in the sand to relieve the pressure of his trainer pushing into his thigh.

"Ah. Yeah, I've been having some too." A cheeky grin opened up on her face. "Do yours go something like this?" She leaned in and pushed her lips against his.

Ray didn't have to be asked twice. He gripped Mina by the hips and turned her so that she straddled him. Her hands roamed his back and came to rest on his chest as her tongue plundered his mouth. Ray fumbled searching for the edge of her knee-length summer dress. His hands scrunched the fabric until it sat bunched around her hips and then he paused.

Leaning back, he faced her confused expression. "Baby. I'm not sure we're ..."

"Shh." She placed an index finger on his mouth as her other hand dove between his legs.

"I don't have a condom."

Mina blushed as she bit her bottom lip. Her innocent gaze caused his need to push uncomfortably against his shorts.

"Then we'll just have to make do." She wiggled down his lap, but Ray stopped her.

"Baby, are you sure? You're overwhelmed, and vulnerable and—"

"I'm a grown woman. Last night, I was vulnerable. Right now ... I need you." She tugged at his shorts, her hungry consent rocking his world off its axis.

His hard-on jumped from its restraints as Mina leaned forward, taking it in her hands. "Fuck, I missed you."

Ray glanced around. Thank God the mist gave them some protection.

Mina slid back and bent over.

"Aaah," he groaned as she licked and flicked the tip

of her tongue around his hard length. Ray grabbed a handful of her hair as she worked him with her mouth. His hunger building, building ... He pulled her away as he reached the edge.

"What?" Her eyes were at half-mast, her tone as hot as her strawberry-red tongue sliding across her plump coral lips.

"I want us to come together." He slipped a hand around her bum and tugged at her cotton panties. She let go of him, stood, and slipped them off before straddling him once more. Taking his hand, she slipped it between her thighs.

"Sweet fuck, you're as slick as a seal, baby."

"Only you've ever done that to me." Her heated words washed over him.

He paused and searched her face.

"There's been no one else since you." She placed one hand on his cheek as she gripped him in her other.

Elation, relief, and a demon's desire surged through his body at her confession.

Slipping two fingers inside of her and placing a thumb on her nub, Ray's hand rode her as hard as hers rode him. She threw her head back.

"Look at me, baby," he ordered, and she complied.

He held her gaze as they worked each other into a frenzied climax. Mina slammed her mouth onto his as they came, groaning their relief together.

———

MINA CLOSED her eyes and allowed the peace of the moment to blanket them where they lay in each other's arms on the sand. She'd come down to the beach for some fresh air and wide open space. Her mind and spirit had been overwhelmed with everything that had happened over the last few weeks. She needed some me time, to digest, and figure out her next steps. She had to face a future with Ray in it, and accept that there was a possibility that both her trusted manager and a woman who'd come knocking on her door, begging for a piece job so that she may feed her and her son, were possibly backstabbing thieves. Her mind still balked at the thought.

So much for second chances.

Mina sat up. "I'd better get back before someone comes looking."

"Yeah, that goes for the both of us." Ray followed her action.

They stood and dusted sand from their limbs before righting their cloths, "Can't say the beach is the most comfortable place to do this," Ray joked.

Mina shook her head. "Yeah, I got sand in you-don't-wanna-know places."

They both erupted in laughter before catching their breaths. Mina stopped and stepped toward him. She cupped his face. "I missed us so much."

"Do you regret it?" Ray placed his hands over hers.

She bit her bottom lip. "Never," She rose on her toes and placed a kiss on his lips.

"Where to from here?" His question mirrored her thoughts.

She shrugged. "Like I said this morning, one step at a time?"

"It does feel like we've skipped a few steps." Ray smiled down at her.

"I need to figure out how *we*"—she waved an index finger between them—"won't interfere with you completing the program. You're still under court order." She slipped her hand into his, and the pair began the walk back to the farm's beach entrance.

"Things okay back at camp?." Mina asked.

"It's good. I want to make a success of this Mina. It's important to me to not skip any steps." Ray squeezed her hand in reassurance.

"Agreed." She stopped and tugged on his arm so that he faced her, "I'm proud of you."

Ray's face turned a subtle pink, "I don't think I've earned that yet. But thanks."

They strode on then came to stand facing the water.

"I need to know." Ray broke the silence. "Was there anything ever between you and Ben?"

Mina shook her head, "Geez, that obvious? No. But yes, I've been aware of his feelings for me. It'll be one of the obstacles we'll need to overcome." She tugged again and they continued to walk. "But he's a good man, Ray. I need him if Redemption is to move on from here." God, she hoped it all worked out and that Ben wasn't who Thomas suspected he was.

"Okay." Ray nodded, and Mina relished the small pocket of relief tucked in his reply.

Their walk continued in silence until they reached the entrance. A fuming Ben pacing its width.

"And just where the fuck ..." He began until his eyes landed on their clasped hands.

"Ben." Mina let go of Ray's hand and stepped toward him.

Ray remained where he stood. It wasn't his place to do or say anything, even if the urge to smack Meintjies stomped like a wounded buffalo in his gut.

"After everything this piece of shit has done to you and Lullu ... how could you just spread your legs—"

Ben didn't get to complete his sentence. Ray balled his fists and stepped forward. But Mina beat him to it as she pulled back her right arm and let fly. Her flat hand connected with Ben's cheek in a resounding crack.

"That ends now, Benjamin Meintjies. I'll see you up at my office."

Ben didn't react to her slap, but merely glared at Ray, spun around, and marched toward the farmhouse.

"I'm sorry," Ray whispered.

"Enough, Ray. You've apologised and now it's done. Get back to your cabin. I'll see you tomorrow."

Ray nodded reluctantly. What she asked of him

wasn't easy, but right then, she needed to lay down the law or chaos would follow.

———

RAY STOMPED INTO HIS ROOM. Cyril lay on his bed, reading a well-used porno mag.

"Where you've been?" The man glanced over the edge of the book.

"Running."

"*Ja*, well Mr Meintjies was looking for you. Seems you like to poke the bear, *ne*." Cyril chuckled.

"Seems so." Ray grabbed clean clothes, his towel, and toiletries.

"*Ja*, well take some good advice, sonny boy. Stay away from the boss and keep your head down. If Mr Meintjies decides to make life hard for all of us because of you, I can't protect you."

Ray paused and gave Cyril his hardest, coldest stare. "Never asked you to."

"Fine. Don't say I didn't try warn you."

13

MINA STOOD AT THE TOP OF THE HILL WHICH GAVE HER A view over the vast Atlantic.

Sun sprites danced on its rolling waves, and in the distance, a pod of dolphins played silly buggers, surfing the applauding waves as they clapped against the shore.

Summer was on its way, and she thrilled at the feel of the hot sun enveloping her. How blessed she was. She, a coloured woman, a single mother—for now— owned one of the most productive abalone farms in South Africa. She also ran the most successful offender rehabilitation centre on the entire continent.

Mina's gaze coveted her kingdom. Yes, here she was king, queen, and ruler. She'd be damned if any arse- holes dared to try and take it from her.

Her eyes grazed over the warehouses and came to land on the inmate living quarters.

The week had come and gone and she was no closer to resolving any of the issues plaguing Redemption. Though she'd tried to stay away after their meeting on the beach, she couldn't help herself and had gone in search of Ray the very next day.

So much for one step at a time—she was practically leapfrogging her way toward another broken heart.

She and Ray had figured out that the time after work and before dinner was best for their clandestine snogs. And the best place was the old maid's quarters on the far side of the house, neatly ensconced by the large, ever-blooming bougainvillea. It housed a lot of old boxes, and an old bed.

Really, she was acting like an impulsive teen again, but she couldn't help it. All common sense fled her adult self-control when it neared that time of the day.

Seagulls drifted on the ocean breeze as a sailboat bobbed across the bay. Was it finally time for her to be absolutely happy? Yes she was worried about Becky and her son somehow being complicit in the poaching, but there were more important people in her life now. Would her greatest fear come to life—would Ray fail them once again?

Her heart and her body ached for him. They should've held steadfast and kept some distance—mainly to prevent painting a target on his back, although she suspected it was too late for that any way.

"Hello Mommy. It's time, or can I go on my own?"

Lullu, still in school uniform, called as she jogged across the lawn.

"Wait right there young lady." Mina summoned her best, don't you mess with me, tone, and her daughter skidded to a halt.

She looked once more over the waters and closed her eyes, 'God give me strength." She whispered in to the breeze.

Turning she walked over to her daughter and the pair stood at the top of the steps separating the camp from the farm house.

"Do you think he forgot?" Lullu bounced up and down where she stood.

Mina bit the inside of her cheek, Ben was probably holding him up with some mundane task in retaliation to her arrangement. Plucking her phone from her jacket Mina quickly sent and message to her farm manager.

"Look, here he comes." Mina pointed a few moments later as Ray came trotting toward them and up the steps.

"Sjoe! Sorry I'm late."

"It's okay. You're here now." Lullu grinned, " Come. Cook has made us a special first lunch. I hope you like gammon and rye bread?" Lullu motioned for her father to follow.

Ray paused and glanced at Mina, "It's alright. Vestra will join you this first time and I'll leave the two of you alone." She gave him her broadest smile.

"Okay." He nodded, turned and trotted after his daughter toward the house.

Lullu had nagged every day after the storm for permission to see her dad. Eventually, Mina had relented and between her and Vestra, they'd come up with a suitable plan – not that Ben had liked it one bit.

"Mina!" Ben's voice echoed up from the camp below. She turned and waved as he hurried up the stairs.

"Hi Ben." She forced a smile.

"Hi yourself. Are you really going ahead with this?" he waved toward the house.

"Yes."

"What about the rules?" he placed his balled hand on his hips.

"There are no rules against this Ben."

"look here..." her wagged a finger in front of her face.

Mina's chest tightened and her temper snapped, "No you look Ben Meintjies, this matter has nothing to do with you. Vestra and I have it under control. Now, if you would please return to your duties in the camp." Mina spun around and walked away. Shit that was not how she'd wanted any of this to go down, but Ben had a way of forcing her into corners she did not like.

Mina stood just outside the kitchen door. Inside Ray and Lullu sat, sandwich in hand, talking. Vestra sat at the far side on a stool pretending to scroll through her phone. None could see Mina where she stood.

"Are you done with being a bad man?" Lullu's direct question had Mina gasping and Ray chocking on his mouthful.

He gripped the glass and downed half his soda. He wiped the back of his hand across his mouth.

"You have a serviette for that. Ma always calls me a philistine when I do it." Lullu handed Ray a white napkin.

"Thanks. And yes, I'm done with all of that." He replied then sat back in his chair.

"Will you stay here when you're done with the program?"

Ray chuckled and nodded his head.

"It's not meant to be funny." Lullu's retort had him looking her right in the eye.

"If you'll have me."

"Do you still love my mom?" she didn't give the man a chance to think as she peppered him with questions. Questions Mina knew she had a right to ask, but she did feel a little sorry for Ray who answered them as best he could.

"Always." His tone was warm and Mina loved how his answer made her heart flutter and her daughters face light up.

But then Lullu's face creased in a deep frown, "An-and me?"

In a split second, her teenager had morphed into a small girl. Naïve, vulnerable and completely innocent. Mina braced herself.

"You, Lullu Marie, are my everything. I love your mother, but I live for you!"

Her daughter wiped her eyes, "And you are mine daddy."

Mina had to walk away as a sob fell from her lips. God almighty!

Mina crouched against the retaining wall which formed a courtyard at her back door. She dug into her back pocket for her tissue and wiped her eyes when a hand touched her shoulder.

"Vestra! Good God, you gave me a fright."

"Spying, are you? I thought it was decided you'd not get involved in this." her friend and stand-in counsellor chided jokingly.

Mina shrugged. "Well ..."

"I understand. They're getting along like a house on fire. She's quite something," Vestra complimented.

"I think I'll go for a walk. I have much to think about." Mina smiled and left.

She inhaled deeply, her chest drawing in the oxygen without any fuss, for the first time in days. Shutting her eyes she stretched her arms to the sides of her body. She was blessed!

Rounding the side of the house, she made her way back to her study to finish off the last of the Progress reports.

Boesman was lazily grazing in his paddock at the far end of the stables. Nationals were creeping closer, and her daughter had to focus. Mina had feared that the recent development would cause a distraction, but her daughter was taking life in her stride, proving otherwise.

Mina made her way through the side sliding door of her home and came to stand in the large open living area. Closing her eyes, she could almost picture him in it. His rustic scent. The sound of his laughter. Spending an evening on the couch with him, watching movies and eating junk food ...

She shouldn't rush things. She was too involved in her feelings and not listening to her common sense. Shaking her head at herself, she made her way to her study.

Sitting down at her desk, she banished all thoughts of Ray and got to work.

———

MINA SLIPPED the key into her desk drawers, saddened by the fact that she had to make a point of keeping her business under lock and key, but hopefully only until the poachers were caught.

More and more, this was the way of life in South Africa. Trust in those one would have given so easily in the past faded like a distant dream.

There'd been no further sign or news of the poachers, and for now, her life was returning to its normal pace—except that Ray was back in it.

Thomas and Rochelle had headed into town for

the day. Thomas wanted to get a feel for the locals as he kept his eyes peeled for anything that could help his investigation, which frustratingly had run into a dead end. They'd promised to stay an extra few nights before heading back to Simon's Town.

"Hey, you got a moment?" Thomas's head popped around her half-open door.

"Geez!" Mina slapped her hands to her chest. "Thought you two were out galivanting."

"Sorry. Didn't mean to scare you. We just got back. I wanted to chat with you quickly."

Mina waved Thomas in and he came to sit at her desk.

"I had a search done on Ben's background and came up with information I think you might already have." He handed Mina a folder.

She bristled but kept quiet as she paged through it. Ben should not be a suspect.

"There's nothing here that I don't already know." She handed the folder back to Thomas.

"I didn't think so. But Mina, he was a dealer. Dealers have contacts and know how to blend in and move under the radar."

Mina bit back her retort. Thomas was, after all, looking out for her and only doing his job.

"And the other folder?" She nodded toward it, lying on her desk.

"Becky and Klein Piet." He flipped it open to reveal a page of scribbled notes. "There's nothing. But this is

South Africa, and unlike in the rest of the world, not every Tom, Dick, and Harry has access to smart phones and social media. And some people are too clever to leave a trail. Contrary to worldly belief, more births and deaths go unregistered than the government would like; not to mention there is a large amount of illegals in the country."

"You think they're from Zimbabwe or Nigeria?" Mina glanced up from the one-pager Thomas had handed to her.

"They don't come across as Nigerians. Too light-skinned, and they speak damn good Xhosa and Zulu."

"Nam? They definitely don't speak any of our local lingos except for Afrikaans." The Namibian border was on their doorstep; it wouldn't be that hard for someone to slip through.

"Don't know. The possibilities are endless," Thomas replied, leaning back and folding his arms across his chest.

"But this doesn't mean they're guilty." Mina shook her head.

"It does give them the anonymity with which to move about undetected, Mina." Thomas jabbed the tip of his index finger onto the desk. "I'm no stranger to this type of criminal. They come in all shapes and sizes. Unfortunately, they're also bloody good at evading authorities—too many corrupt government contacts." Thomas folded his hands on the desk, then gave her a sincere look.

"How are things developing between you and Raymond?" He cut straight to his next question, and a blush rose up her neck and hugged her cheeks.

"We're, erm ..."

"I'd hate to have to sound like the parent but ..." He held up both his hands. "... I've noticed that Ben and some of the inmates are making it their priority to make life difficult for him. They know of his connection to you and that he disappears every afternoon."

Mina's gaze dropped to the floor, then shot back up. Why in the hell should she feel chastised?

"Ray's a big boy. He can deal. But if you notice the situation escalating, let me know and I'll make a plan. He has to serve his time." Mina decided on a more logical than emotional-based reply.

"I hear you. And Lullu. Has she ...?"

Mina smiled. "Well, she's made a point of getting to know him. I've also arranged a sit-down with the three of us and Vestra. After all the years spent not knowing a peep about her missing father, she's suddenly OCD, having to learn everything."

Thomas chuckled. "I suppose that's a child for you."

"Well, Lullu's reached Inquisitive 2.0. 'When will Daddy leave the program? Can Daddy come and watch me at nationals? It'd be so cool if Daddy could join us for Sunday lunch when Oupa and Omie are here.'"

"She calls him Daddy?" Thomas cocked an eyebrow.

"Yup." Mina shrugged

"You haven't seen the man in more than a decade. Do you think it's wise?"

"One thing I have learned is that when it comes to matters of the heart, wisdom is rarely involved. At this stage, I'm going with the flow, or trying to." She looked away as memories of her and Ray's tryst resurfaced. "Speaking of ..." Mina decided a change of subject was in order as they both stood and walked out of the study. "Are you and Rochelle planning to expand your family?"

Thomas shrugged. "We're trying. I guess it'll happen when it happens. We're not in a rush right now. But yeah, it'd be nice to give Lullu a cousin or two."

Mina drew closed her door and twisted the bronze key in its lock. The door was a wooden frame with a lead glass centre; it'd do little to stop anyone who really wanted to gain entrance, but locking it told her house staff they were being watched.

"Well, why don't you and Rochelle head down to the beach? The day is perfect. I have some issues to deal with." A sit-down with Ben was in order. She had too much respect for the man not to be honest with him—that, and she wanted to look him in the eye when she made it clear for the last time that there would never be anything more than friendship and a working relationship between them.

"If it's confronting your manager, I'd suggest you

don't," Thomas said.

"I won't ask him about the poaching – I just want to clear things up with him about Ray. You don't understand the complex relationship I have with him. I'll tread carefully, I promise." She patted the man's shoulder as she headed out and down to her farm manager's office.

Clenching her fists as she strolled down the garden and steps, she revisited her demons.

Was it at all possible to work toward a future with Ray in it? As her lover and partner, and the father to their daughter? Or was she simply acting like the impulsive teen who'd gotten in over her head all those years ago?

Mina sighed, and rubbed her eyes with the back of her hand. There were no answers—only a plethora of raw, sticky, molasses-like emotions. Was their future filled with pain and indecision, or would she and Ray get through this and just maybe, find their happy every after? Rochelle and Thomas had.

Ugh—there was so much to consider and sort out. She wished she could simply run away with Lullu and Ray to an isolated location with only a house, wine, and the ocean.

Ben's door was closed but his air conditioner was running. Mina walked up to the door and knocked.

"Come in," he called.

Mina stepped inside, closing the door behind her. Ben's office was unlike hers. He had a window looking out onto the ocean, but his wall stood bare, and only a desk, filing cabinet, and three chairs decorated the room's innards.

His face was drawn and his gaze dark. "Sit, please. Coffee? Something stronger?"

She shook her head. "No. You know why I've come."

He nodded solemnly. "Let's get this over with." His tone resigned, he folded his hands on his lap and looked at his feet.

"Ben. Please look at me?"

The man hesitated, then slowly raised his head until his empty, sad eyes found hers.

"I never meant for you to get hurt. I've always told you where you stand with me."

"I know." He nodded.

"You've always had my and Lullu's best interests at heart, but ..." She paused.

"So what happens if he completes his time here?"

Mina's brain homed in on Ben's use of the word *if*. "That's between me and Ray."

"And what happens to me?" Ben's tone hardened.

"I hope you will stay. I need you. Redemption needs you ..."

"Pfft." He rose from his chair and walked over to his window, hands tucked in his pockets. "I'm not sure I want to. If anything, I deserve time to sort my own future out, Mina. But don't expect me to go light on that man just 'cause he's your lover." He turned and leaned on the back of his chair. His eyes burned with pain and anger.

A thread of fear wound its way around Mina's heart. His words caused her to second guess her fighting for him to stay. "I don't. But I also expect more integrity from you as a manger and a leader, Ben." She made sure her words drove home her meaning, and her tone made it clear she'd not tolerate his childish bullshit.

Ben nodded, straightened himself, and sat. "If that's all, I have reports to complete and get to you."

Mina stood a few more moments as silence embedded itself between them. Ben glanced at his computer screen, he was obviously done discussing the situation. Mina turned and left.

Outside, workers and inmates were busy with their duties. The sun bore down on the earth, and the waves crashed loudly as they spat driftwood and used shells on to the beach. Mina walked along the strand instead of through the warehouses on her way back to the farmhouse.

Was there a future with both Ray and Ben on the farm? She didn't know anything right now—and that irked her.

Was Thomas right about his suspicions? This, she couldn't even begin to conceptualise. Either way, until proven otherwise, and whether Ben wanted it or not, she had his back. As for Becky and Klein Piet, she had no idea.

14

"Sis says they've hit a dead end in the investigation," Ray whispered as he traced the line of vertebrae down Mina's bareback. The pair lay on a picnic blanket, spread over the old bed.

He'd had a hard time getting away this afternoon. Ben finding one aimless job after another for him to do when all the other inmates were on free time.

It'd been Thomas asking to chat with Ben that had eventually given him the gap to escape.

"I'm pleased to hear you and Rochelle are on speaking terms," Mina said.

"It's awkward, but yeah. It was Vestra's idea." Ray shook his head at the memory of Rochelle sitting with her legs and arms crossed, squinting at him suspiciously as Vestra suggested they try and discuss their tumultuous history.

"Mmm, coulda guessed. Vessies's turning out to be

one of my better decisions." Mina turned her head so that her cheek rested on her hands.

Ray sucked in a breath at her words. Did she believe she was making a mistake with him?

Split seconds of wordless moments froze between them.

"I'm not sure how I feel about it all," Mina continued. "It's frustrating and frightening all at once. Who do I trust ... Who can I trust?"

Oh, she meant the poachers. *Thank goodness.*

"Patience. They'll slip up sooner or later. I'll keep my ears close to the ground." He wanted her to know he wasn't the Ray from fourteen years ago and that she could trust him. He also knew that it wouldn't be an easy task to prove. "I'll never let you down again."

Mina opened her eyes. Her gaze was intense, searching, uncertain. Lifting her head, she reached out and touched his cheek, her lips parted as she pulled him to her. His mouth touched hers. Her kiss soothed the awkward silence stirring between them.

Ray shifted so that his body came to lie between her legs, his chest on her back.

"We can't go on like this either, Ray." She twisted her head and spoke over her shoulder.

"What do you suggest?" He began trailing kisses across her shoulders and on her neck as he pushed her legs farther apart with his own, reaching for a foil packet at the same time.

Mina groaned as he bit and tore open the condom and slipped it on.

"Later," he whispered as he slid inside of her.

Ray placed both his palms flat on the bed beside her as he moved, slowly, in and out.

"God, Ray. You're killing me." Her groan increased his hunger for her.

She tucked her head in as her hands grabbed the blanket and she pushed up on her knees, forcing her arse back and giving him deeper access.

Ray gripped her thigh and arched his neck; timing was everything. He alternated between slow and hard.

"I'm gonna come," she mewled.

Ray slowed right down. Every inch of him wanted to take her, but his longing to have her wrapped around him for longer won.

"Not yet, baby." He pulled out, cupping her breast, then allowing his fingers to find their way between her legs. She rose with her back against his front. Ray thrilled in cupping his free hand around the front of her neck as the other worked her.

"Just fuck me again already," she begged.

Ray smiled. God, how he'd missed her. Pushing her onto all fours, and with a measured force, he ploughed back into her, pulled out, and slammed in again.

Soon, his own need overrode his want for taking it slow. Ray pumped in and out until he had to bury his face in her hair that lay bunched around her neck. She groaned into the blanket. They were good at reaching their climax together, and there was nothing like her hungry, wet walls clamping down on him as he came.

They lay panting on their backs.

"We need to get ready. It's our turn with Vestra before dinner." Mina eventually rose, grabbing her lace underwear, T-shirt, and three-quarter pants.

"Do we have to? Lullu and I are getting along nicely. I feel like all I'm doing is sitting in counselling sessions these days." Ray reached out and pulled her to him.

"Yes. I'm not taking any chances, Ray. For her. We have to do this the right way." She cupped his face and planted a kiss on his forehead, and Ray slipped his clothes back on.

After making sure there was no one about, Ray sprinted from their hideout and down the steps, only stopping when he reached the bottom. Footsteps behind him caused him to turn. His heart jumped into his throat as Ben sauntered toward him.

"Best get to your meeting then." Ben's words were cold and his eyes were dark.

Ray nodded and walked off.

Fuck!

———

"Come, sit." Vestra waved him in.

Ray's heart thumped against its cage as it always did when he got to chat with his daughter. He wiped his palms down his work uniform. He'd thought to keep them on. They looked neater than his well-worn jeans and trainers, and he wanted to make an impression.

"Hi Dad." Lullu smiled up at him from her chair. Her words warmed that hollow spot in his chest.

"Hello Lovie."

"Ma, can I hug him?" Lullu stepped toward Ray, who wasn't sure if he should turn and run away, or …

"Erm, Lullupops, maybe …" Mina didn't get a chance to finish her sentence as Lullu, stepped forward, and wrapped her arms around Ray.

Lullu's head reached just below his chest and her arms didn't quite make it all the way around his torso.

This child marched to the beat of her own drum. For the shortest moment, Ray felt sorry Mina had to contend with a teenage will on her own, but then he remembered that Mina was much the same.

"That feels good, and you smell just like the sea. I like that." She spoke into his shirt.

Ray swallowed hard.

Would it be appropriate to cry in front of his daughter? Helluva impression that'd make. He allowed his arms to snake around her as he lowered his head and placed a gentle kiss on the golden crown of her hair. Everything that had ever been broken inside of him came together. Both the jagged and the sharp melded to form a whole which had lain shattered for many years.

"Thank you, Lovie. You smell like horses and spring blossoms." He glanced at Mina, not sure if he was saying the right thing.

Mina smiled and nodded, easing the tension building in his gut. This wasn't their first visit, but he

Lullu giggled as she let go. "Agh, it's probably Boesman's hay you're smelling, but I love the smell of horses too."

"Well, now that the ice is broken, shall we begin?" Vestra brought the emotional meeting to order with her warm, therapeutic voice.

"Oh, I think the ice has been broken for a while now." Mina chuckled as she shook her head and sat.

"Yes, so it has. You've been luncheoning with your dad this last week, haven't you? So Lullu, I guess the main reason we're here is to find out how you're coping with all of this new ... stuff?" Vestra said.

"If you're asking if I'm like Sara at school, nope. I'm fine, thank you." Lullu pinched her hands between her jodhpur-clad knees, her eyes bright and warm like her mother's.

A deafening silence descended as Ray looked first to Vestra then Mina.

"And what is happening with Sara?" Vestra leaned back in her chair, sliding one leg under her bum and creating a comfortable and informal feel to the conversation.

"Agh, she doesn't know who her pa is, and some of

the kids are meanies!" Lullu's eyes darted to Ray, then settled on Mina.

"Have you been teased?" Mina leaned forward, the lines in her forehead creasing deeply.

"They tried to," she confessed looking at her feet then back up.

Mina's eyes widened as she straightened, "Why didn't you tell me? Was that when Mr Dempsey called me in because you *bliksemed* that kid?"

He glanced back at Lullu, who was swallowing hard. His absence had caused his daughter pain.

"*Ja*, Ma. And no one's tried to give me shit since."

"Lullu Marie van der Westhuizen, you mind that mouth of yours, girl," Mina chastised.

"Sorry, Ma."

Ray bit back a smile and scraped together his courage. "Erm ..." He stood, then sat again, not knowing where to look or put his hands and legs. "Lovie, I'm sorry you got teased because I am such a crap father."

Lullu's head snapped toward him and a large, starry smile opened up her sweet, beautiful face. "Agh, Daddy, don't be silly. We tease each other all the time at school, and sometimes when it gets too much, we sort it out—or some of us do." She glanced at Mina who sat eyes wide, staring at their daughter.

. . .

"So why do you think it no longer upsets you? The teasing, that is," Vestra said.

"It never really did. Well, not after Oupa told me that people usually get ugly when they are jealous, so I figured it was because I have my mommy, live on this farm and have a horse—that's why they were mean. I invited them over to visit, you know, so I could share some of my happiness with them. But they just got uglier so I figured they could do with a small attitude adjustment."

Ray cupped his mouth in his hand to hide his grin.

"I always knew you would come back. Mommy never told me where you went, but I knew if Oupa was around, you would come home one day."

Vestra glanced down at her notepad as she scribbled, trying to hide her smile, and Mina beamed through her tears.

"Lullu ..." Mina said.

"I also found a photo of you and Dad when you were younger," Lullu confessed.

Both Ray and Mina looked at each other, then to Lullu.

"I knew you were my dad. I have your hair." She tugged on her ponytail. "And Ma looks happy now, like she did in the photo."

Lullu's words nearly brought Ray to his knees. *Out of the mouths of babes.*

"I prayed every night that Mommy would find you again. She needed to be loved. She was always loving everyone else and protecting everyone else. She needs you to do that for her now. You're not a bad dad; you were just acting up, like I do sometimes too." A cheeky grin was proffered to Mina, who simply chuckled through her tears.

Ray leaned across and wiped them away with his thumb. "And I promise you that is what I'll do." His voice broke.

"So, will Daddy move in to your room now?"

———

THEY LEFT Ray to return to the now repaired mess hall for dinner with the remaining inmates. She'd only six of them left, but the good news was this looked to be the largest graduating success in the history of her rehab centre.

Lullu's final question still rippled through Mina like a lost electrical current searching for its earth, as they approached her home.

"Thank you." Mina wrapped an arm around her friend's shoulders as she and Vestra watched Lullu bolt up the steps toward the farmhouse.

"It's only a pleasure, but Mina ..."

They stopped and Mina sighed. "I know. I'll be careful."

Vestra smiled. "You've changed many people's lives here at Redemption, but just because you love him, don't allow it to blind you."

"Is there something I need to know?" Mina's stomach lurched.

"No. From the work I've been doing with Ray, I can honestly say he is giving it his best shot, and fuck me, I wish I had someone who looked at me the way he does at you. But there's always that chance. He'll always be an addict. There will always be a darkness waiting to pounce."

Mina nodded as they continued their way up the steps. "I know. But I also know that no one person is perfect, and this time, he won't face that darkness alone."

15

RAY STOOD BESIDE LULLU THE NEXT MORNING, AS MINA walked out with Rochelle and Thomas. She was sad to see them go. She was really getting to know Rochelle on a different level and found that she enjoyed having family, because after everything that had happened, that was what they'd become.

"I'm sorry I wasn't much help. But please remember I'm on the case," Thomas said as he walked toward his double cab *bakkie*, placing his and Rochelle's suitcase on the back seat.

"It's fine. I just hope you guys get them before they pounce again." Mina opened her arms when Rochelle walked towards her, and wrapped her arms around her.

"Christmas, our place," she reminded Mina.

"No!" Lullu's sharp scream caused them all to spin around.

Ben had Ray in a headlock with one of the security guards raining down blows on Ray with a baton. Ray struggled and almost broke free.

"Ben, what the fuck!" Mina shouted as she sprinted toward her daughter, pushing aside Lullu, who'd been in the throes of slapping and kicking her farm manager, trying to free her dad.

"Let me handle this, Mina. It's my job," Ben commanded as he placed a thick black restraint around Ray's wrists and pulled so tight his fingertips immediately turned blue.

Ray attempted to pull away. "What is this?" he shouted as the guard punched him in the gut.

"Enough!" Mina shot a hand toward the guard, connecting her flat palm to his cheek. "I'll have your job for this."

"We found contraband in his room," Ben explained Thomas strode toward them.

Ray, panting, saliva streaked across his face, fell to his knees and shook his head. "Impo—impossible."

"*Shurrup*, you." Ben shoved his foot against Ray's ribs.

"Touch him again ..." Mina took a menacing step forward.

"It's okay," Ray managed as Ben forced him to his feet then shoved him into the clutches of the accompanying guard.

"It's not true, lovie," he called to Lullu.

Ben back-handed him and Lullu screamed.

"Ben!" Mina shouted.

"What, Miss van der Westhuizen? I'm doing what you pay me to do!"

"I do not pay you to abuse our inmates!" she yelled.

"Mind I don't have reason to use those restraints on you, Benjamin." Thomas took over, gently pushing Mina behind him and into his wife's arms. "Where are you taking him?"

"He'll be confined to his cabin until prison services can collect him."

"I'll sort this out." Thomas placed a hand on Ray's shoulder, then looked up to Ben. "I'll be accompanying you to make sure the inmate makes it to his cabin safely."

———

THOMAS WALKED in to the kitchen to find Mina and Rochelle sitting at the table sipping coffee, which smelled an awful lot like it had some brandy involved, "How is Lullu?"

"Sleeping. Rochelle ..." Mina trembled as she tried to lift her mug to her lips but gave up after spilling half its contents. "... gave her a mild sedative. I've asked Vestra if she'd do a sit-down with her tomorrow."

Thomas dropped a sealed plastic bag on the table. "This is what Ben found in Ray's bedroom tucked beneath his mattress."

Mina glanced down at the bag. "*Dube*? And what are those pills?"

"*Khat.*"

"Shit! His drug of choice," Rochelle spat.

"Babes. We don't know for sure. I need you to go down and take a urine and blood sample from him. Something about all this doesn't sit right with me." Thomas sat at the table and took his wife's hand in his.

"He's done a backslide is what's happened." Rochelle's bitter voice cut in to Mina.

"Rochelle, please. I believe Thomas. Something is out of place here. Please help me find out if Ray is in trouble." Mina said.

"And if he tests positive?" Rochelle placed her mug on the table.

"We'll get him through this." Mina forced away her angry tears. She would. She'd not leave him to the wolves a second time. But she'd also have to rethink her relationship with him if his drug habit was getting the better of him. Under no circumstances could she ever expose Lullu to it.

Mina gripped a hand to her stomach. She'd hoped for too much, fallen all over again, and here she sat, reaping the rotten harvest of her impulsive harvest for a second time. But for now, she had to hold on to the glimmer of hope in her centre.

"The guys know their rooms are searched every day. Why would he hide it under his mattress? There are so many other places. All the inmates who've ever had a backslide hid their stash in the warehouses. One even buried it in my garden," Mina explained.

Rochelle stood. "Don't tell Pa— not until we know for sure. I'll grab my bag and arrange with the path lab for a priority pick-up." She turned and walked out.

"Come. He needs us both down there, and your employees need to know you're in charge, not Ben, or something ugly could go down." Thomas stood just as Becky strode in.

"Afternoon, madam." Becky quickly folded her hands behind her back, crumpling a piece of paper in her hand.

"Hi Becky, I'd like you to fetch cook please? And then you can have the afternoon off." It wasn't missed by Mina that she looked a bit jumpy. But, Mina didn't care.

She no longer trusted this woman, and until Thomas found evidence confirming that she was innocent or complicit, Mina would not leave her alone with Lullu.

"Do you think she suspects you no longer trust her?" Rochelle said.

"I hope not. But if it's that obvious to you..."

"It's only because I am privy to Thomas investigation." Rochelle reassured her, "Cook is a good woman. Lullu will be safe."

———

Ray didn't bother confessing his innocence as he sat at the table while his sister prepared her needle and tubes. Her face spoke volumes, and if she thought he was guilty, well then ...

A commotion from outside distracted them both from their dark silence.

"You don't need bloods. They can do that back in prison. We found the evidence, and that's all that's needed," Ben roared.

Ray bit his tongue. That goddamned prick had framed him. No wonder he didn't want bloods and urine done here. He'd make sure Ben got his payday. He dreamed of planting a few choice jabs in the moth-erfucker's face for upsetting Lullu the way he had. As for Mina? The pain in her eyes? Ray shook his head.

"Sit still, will you." Rochelle gripped his arm and slid the needle in. "I'm still pissed at you. But the fact that that man's arguing so hard to get you gone ..." She removed the needle and shoved a cotton ball on the area she'd just pierced. "Hold this down." She inserted the needle into a tube and injected his withdrawn blood into it. "I hope to fuck you're innocent, 'cause if you've hurt that little girl and Pa ..."

"I am." He pushed down on the wad, not looking up at her.

Rochelle packed the clean kidney dish, sterile needles, tubes and other tools she needed back in to her medical bag. She proceeded to label the tubes as Thomas and Mina stepped inside. The urge to kneel at

Mina's feet and plead his innocence burned his insides as he looked into her dark, sad eyes.

"You'll be safe in here. I have one of my most trusted men outside," she explained as Thomas and Rochelle left them alone.

"I swear, baby ..."

"Whatever the outcome, I won't let you do this on your own, okay?" Her words were sincere but the fact that she didn't come closer, wrap herself around him, cut deep and put the fear of the almighty in him.

"Lullu?" It was all he could muster.

"She's okay for now," Mina replied softly, "Look, keep your head down. As soon as we get the results, we can clear this all up."

"You believe me?" Hope's flame re-ignited.

Mina nodded, but her eyes still entertained doubt.

"I'll come down before dinner," she promised and slipped out.

Ray's skin puckered at the sound of the lock snapping shut.

Here he was, once again in a prison, and this time it wasn't of his own making.

He slumped onto his bed. Why now? Life had finally been looking up, and he'd been moving forward. Was this his fate? To always be the bad man? The down-on-his-luck man? The useless father?

His craving resurfaced and Ray groaned as he leaned forward, harnessing all his coping skills to fight it. He broke out in a cold sweat and his skin began to crawl. No! He wasn't going to give in. Besides, there was nothing in his room to get high on in any case.

A thought struck. He stumbled over to his desk, opened it, and pulled out his writing pad and pen.

Writing had been like opening a floodgate; the words simply flowed. Perhaps sorting his thoughts out on paper might prove to be the elixir for his dilemma.

Bossy, loud, demanding,

His pen scribbled across the page.

Needy, hungry, angry
The devil seeks his due,
No longer will a bargain make do
Bridges built he yearns to burn,
One snort, one draw, one needles sanction ...

The lock of his cabin door clicked, and the door swung open.

In the entrance stood Ben, wearing a smirk so wide Ray ached to wipe it off his face with the sole of his shoe.

"Here. I know this is all you need." He chucked the baggy onto the floor and slammed the door shut. So much for Mina's trusted employee.

Ray sat on his bed, eyeing the baggy as though it were a large spider about to pounce.

Writing forgotten, his hunger grew.

They've already taken your bloods. Who's gonna know? Just one hit, boet. *You need something to get you through this."*

The voices of old made themselves known one by one.

Bile etched its way up his gullet and sat in the back of his throat, burning, boiling, gnawing.

After an eternity, Ray jumped off his bed toward the parcel which screamed at him to pick it up and enjoy what it had to offer.

he slid across the floor in his socks, Ben having removed his shoes, belt, and anything else they deemed he could possibly use to self-harm.

Kneeling, he picked up the bag of drugs and utensils. His hand shook violently as he peeled open the bag, dipped his head and inhaled.

Lullu and Mina's faces danced across his conscience.

Clutching the baggie in his fist he leaned back, then with all his might, threw it at the opposite wall. The pipe shattered and the packet dropped onto the bed where Cyril usually slept until Ben had moved him out.

"I will not give in!" Ray screamed, hoping Ben was listening.

Ray summarily dropped to the floor and began doing push-ups, then sit-ups, then shadow boxing ... Anything and everything he could to rid his mind and body of the evil threatening to take hold.

The sun was setting outside, throwing the room in dark shadows which moved and bobbed. Ray paced the width of the small cabin.

The cabin was hot, the burglar-proofed window open, but no breeze drifted in. There'd been no lunch, and there was no water. He'd banged against his door, demanding he be fed and given something to drink. Ben had answered, smacked him, grabbed the smashed baggy, and walked back out.

Shit. His only hope was Mina. But even she'd not come down, and judging by the low-hanging sun, it was well after seven and dinnertime. What the fuck was going on?

Ray slumped against the wall, and began to sob. This was it—his last chance blown to smithereens. He was done for—Ben would make sure of it.

"I'll take care of the of the idiot down here and wait on the strand." A voice Ray recognised as his ex-roomie's drifted through the window. "What you lot getting up to, huh?"

"Piet's watching that bitch and her brat. We'll be ready for pick-up at midnight. We need to grab the remaining abalone tonight," a female voice ordered.

"I'll have a skiff ready," Cyril replied.

"Make sure there are no eyewitnesses. What about the guards and other inmates?" Was that Becky's voice?

"Leave it to me. You just do your job, and I'll do mine."

Becky was involved, and something was very wrong up at the farmhouse. Adrenaline surged through his limbs and Ray's mind shifted in to get-out-and-save-my-family mode.

Ray ran to his door and pounded on it again. "Hey, asshole. Want another piece of me?" he yelled, hoping Ben might open up and give him a chance to break out. He wouldn't be able to explain as the fucking oaf was either involved or too full of shit to listen. Either way, it was up to Ray to get out and get up to the house, now!

"Goddammit!" Ray yelled.

It'd been more than half an hour and his shoulders throbbed from all the thumping he'd been giving them against the door. Was Ben truly going to ignore him?

He banged again, and the door unlocked.

Ray stepped back and readied himself to tackle whoever stood in his way.

About to rage like a bull, Ray froze when Thomas slipped inside and closed the door behind him.

"What the fuck Thomas? There's big shi—"

Thomas held up his hand, silencing Ray. "I know. I managed to get out. The idiots think I'm in town. But they've got Mina and Lullu." Thomas put a hand over Ray's mouth when he began to protest. "Shh, dammit. For now, they're unharmed. You, me, and Ben need to get up there, pronto."

"Where's Rochelle?"

"She managed to get away with my phone to call for backup." Thomas said.

"Can't you call the police?"

"Someone in authority is involved. I'm not sure if it's the local police or conservation, so until Rochelle can make the call to my people, we're fucked." Thomas walked over to the door. "We don't have time to waste. Come on."

"Why not use Ben's office phone?"

"All phone lines are cut and they're using jammers, so no cell phones either."

Ray followed Thomas and they made their way to Ben's office.

"Hey, can we trust that asshole?" Ray whispered harshly.

Thomas nodded as they came up to the door.

"How do you know? The fucker planted drugs in my room." Ray pointed to the door angrily.

"I don't think he did. I got a message about one of the inmates just before Becky and Piet attacked. But not now—I don't have time. Ray." Thomas gripped his shoulder. "I need you to trust me."

"Was it Cyril?"

Thomas paused and glanced back at him. "How did you know?"

"I heard them plotting outside my window. Cyril's grabbing the remaining abalone and waiting with a skiff on the beach. I think they're being collected out at sea."

"Okay ... good to know. But first, we need to get the girls free and safe. My people can deal with Cyril and their ride."

Ray nodded. He trusted his brother-in-law. But was Thomas right about Ben?

Thomas let go of Ray's shoulder, and gripped the

door handle and opened it.

"Shit!" Thomas sprinted forward and came to kneel at the side of Ben, who lay groaning and gripping his skull.

"Bloody arseholes. Wait till ..."

"Are you okay to sit up? Mind your hand. Let me see," Thomas instructed with Ray watching the door.

"Fucker came from behind. I think it's that Cyril bloke." Ben grimaced as Thomas inspected his skull.

"Well, I can't see any blood, so hopefully nothing's damaged inside. Can you stand? We need every hand we can get."

"*Ja* ..."

"No time now." Thomas's voice cut Ben off. The bully did a double take and stopped his ranting.

"The poachers are back, and they have Mina and Lullu up at the farmhouse ..."

Ben made a rush to the door.

"Ben, stop!" Thomas pulled rank.

The bulky man skidded to a halt. "You're right. We need to call Abbe."

"For fuck's sake. *Shurrup* and listen!" Ray held up a hand.

Ben squinted at him, but something made him take a deep breath and turn to face Thomas.

"We only get one shot at this," Thomas said.

"Stopping the poachers?" Ben asked.

"No." Thomas shook his head. "At saving the women we all love."

16

LULLU SQUIRMED AGAINST HER RESTRAINTS WHEN KLEIN Piet kneeled before her where she was sat on the cold dining room floor.

Mina screamed against her gag for him to leave her alone, but the cloth slipped deeper into her mouth, causing her to retch. Her lungs began to burn and sweat dripped down the sides of her face.

"I've always looked young for my age. Reckon it's in the genes." Klein Piet wiped a hand across his smooth-as-a-baby's-bottom cheeks. Cheeks Mina wanted to slap silly before she stomped them with her foot.

He reached out and with the same hand, stroked Lullu's hair and face. Her daughter's eyes widened, glanced at her, then looked back at their captor as she kicked out. Piet jumped out the way, Lullu's foot narrowly missing his privates. "Gonna get a lot for you, that's for sure."

Mina screamed and fought her bonds. It was getting harder for her to breathe. Black spots clouded her vision. She had to remain conscious!

"*Shurrup*, bitch." Klein Piet shouted. "Think you the bee's fucking knees with your in-charge attitude. You so loved the timid Klein Piet who needed your strong hand to guide him. Placing me under Baas Ben's wing while my sister ruled your house without you even knowing."

Becky called to him. He spat at Mina, then turned and strode away.

Mina blinked away her tears and shifted her body until she managed to reach Lullu, who sat dead still and was pale as cream.

Try as she might, the plastic restraints that worked like tie-downs wouldn't budge and only cut deeper into her skin the more she fought against them. But she had to do something. They could have all the abalone, burn down the God damned farm too if they pleased, but they'd never get her daughter.

The sound of a car pulling up outside got Mina's already throbbing heart beating faster.

Please, God, let it be Thomas and Rochelle.

Another thought hit her. What if they'd harmed Thomas and Rochelle?

Mina fought against her gag, trying her hardest to push it out of her mouth with her tongue, but to no avail. Then she tried screaming through her nose, which only to caused her to gag again as footsteps and voices came closer.

Mina looked up, and her heart crashed in to her boots.

Marnus Faldela, their local nature conservationist and a man she had trusted, stood looking down at her. Tucked snugly under his arm and grinning down at them was Becky.

"You're brother has a point. We can get a pretty penny for this one, and with the abalone we can wash our hands of the whole bunch and go relax in the Maldives, *liefie*." He pushed the toe of his boot against a shivering Lullu who kicked back, this time hitting her target—his shin.

"*Vok!*" Marnus retracted his arm to slap the child but Mina threw herself in the way, copping the blow.

"Agh. Ever the fucking martyr."

"Leave them, my love." Becky, who was now dressed in a pair of skin-tight jeans, expensive boots and blouse, turned Marnus's head and kissed him.

"Keep some for later when we're done here." He said.

"Come. There's gotta be booze somewhere in this house, and we need to go over the plans. You sure Ben won't come up?"

"No. According to Cyril, he's lights out." Becky nodded in Mina's direction as the pair strode off.

"And the guests?"

"Last I heard, they'd fucked off to town for the night."

"Good ..." Their voices dimmed as they walked away.

Mina's head spun from the slap Marnus had dealt. Her right eye was closing up from the swelling. Lullu leaned forward as if to get her attention.

Mina placed her head against her daughter's to reassure her she was okay when the front door opened and closed again.

Mina and Lullu both stiffened until Rochelle's familiar face peered around the corner, her finger on her lips.

Rochelle tiptoed toward the pair and knelt down, pushing Mina forward and slicing off her restraints, then doing the same to Lullu before helping them get rid of their gags.

Mina gasped for air, coughed into her hands, and gasped again.

's

"My—my office," Mina whispered.

"They're in the kitchen. Klein Piet is out front." Rochelle whispered. "I won't be able to get to your study. Will you be okay?"

"And just where in the hell do you think you're going?" a voice called out.

The scuffling of chairs and pounding feet echoed through the house as Becky and Marnus ran in to the dining room.

Rochelle didn't waste time. "Run, now!" She pushed Lullu to her feet. The small girl darted past Klein Piet, who came running up behind Marnus and Becky. He reached for her daughter and Mina dove on to him.

Lullu's shrill scream echoed through the house and then silence. Klein Piet fought to get Mina off of him, but she managed a knee in the groin where they struggled on the floor, and then smacked his head on the cold floor tiles.

"Enough!" a deep voice called out, and Mina rolled onto her back, her ability to draw in a clean breath worsening. Marnus grabbed Rochelle, and Becky pointed a gun to Mina's sister-in-law's head. Thank God Lullu had gotten away!

"I-I sw-swear, if you killed my *boet* ..." Becky's weapon-loaded hand shook.

"I think he's just passed out." Marnus peered past Rochelle to Piet. Her large blue eyes were wide and fear-filled.

"Come here." He motioned with his head for Mina to get up and walk over to him.

"Ta-take the abalone and go. There's no need for all of this!" Mina wheezed.

"No, but we do love to have our fun. Saw some great work on another farm with an iron. Liefie, go find the iron." He grinned at Becky, who nodded as she handed Marnus the revolver.

Mina rolled over onto her hands and knees, her chest spasmed and burned.

"Yeah, I'd planned on catching up with some extra work today." The look of utter evil which danced in her dark brown eyes caused Mina to retch and clutch her belly.

———

RAY SLOTTED ammunition into the point two-two rifle and readied it for action.

"Know your guns, eh?" Ben commented as he gripped two semi-automatic pistols before sliding them into their holsters on either side of his hips.

"Didn't know ex-crims were allowed gun licenses." Ray slid a cap he took off Ben's table on backward. He smiled inwardly when Ben's nose flared and his mouth pulled askew affirming Ray's suspicions.

"This is South Africa, *boet*. Place a two hundred-rand note in the right hand and you get what you need."

"And what else have you paid for, Ben?" Ray stepped toward him, squaring his shoulders.

Thomas intervened as the two bristled. "Boys. Stay focused. You two cocks can beat the snot out of each other as soon as we've got these fuckers cornered." Thomas slid his pistol into his holster.

"Okay. Give me that scope." Thomas pointed to the item he'd removed from the rifle sitting on Ben's desk.

"Make sure your men and the inmates don't come anywhere near the house," Thomas ordered Ben, and Ray smirked inwardly. He liked seeing the bully of Redemption Farm being told what to do.

"All inmates are in lockdown. Guards know to keep out of the way. They're not trained for this anyway."

Ray snorted, and Thomas held up his hand as a warning to both men.

"Follow me. It's dark enough for us to make it up to the house unseen. Then stay put where I tell you to so I can re-con and get a feel of who's who in the zoo. My people can't be too far off if Rochelle got hold of them."

Thomas waved to the men, who followed him out of Ben's office.

Ray swallowed. He'd only ever killed a buck in his entire life, and while he used to be a pretty good shot back in the day, he hoped his aim had remained true. He had no qualms about pointing and pulling the trigger at the fuckers who had his daughter and Mina.

The trio skulked up the stairs and 'round the side of the house when Thomas held up his hand and motioned for them to lay low as he moved, gripping the scope in his right hand.

It wasn't long until Thomas returned. "For fuck's sake. That goddam woman." He cursed under his breath.

"What—is Mina—"

"Mina is alive. I can't see Lullu, but they have

Rochelle! God damnit, I told her to stay in town!"
Thomas cursed.

"Okay. We have one chance at this. That conservation asshole is with Becky, and Klein Piet is laying passed out on the floor." Thomas held up his hand to silence both Ray and Ben. "The kitchen door is open. Ben, you'll go through there. Ray, you're with me. Wait for our signal before you enter the house, Ben,"

"What's the signal?" Ben asked, his frown deepening.

"You'll know."

Ray followed Thomas as Ben took off toward the kitchen. They stopped short of the glass door leading to the dining room area off the side verandah.

"Okay, we need to distract them. I reckon one rifle shot. Do you think you can wound Marnus?" Thomas pointed to the tallest figure. "And don't miss *boet*; he's got my wife."

"I'm not sure what this rifle is capable of, but I know I can distract them." Ray steadied himself.

No pressure then ...

Ray took aim. It wasn't easy with the scope missing and he hoped the gun's aim wasn't out either.

He kneeled, resting one elbow on his knee, exhaled, and inhaled as he squeezed the trigger.

The shot echoed off across the night sky. Glass shattered and screams accompanied a frenzy of movement. Ray didn't stop to investigate what the *chop, chop, chop* that was making its way closer.

Gripping the rifle, he ran through the remaining glass into the dining room where a screaming Becky stood over the limp body of Ranger Marnus. Becky made to go at him. In one swift move, Ray connected the rifle's butt to her jaw. She dropped like a brick.

Turning toward Rochelle, Thomas and Mina, holding the rifle in one hand, Ray threw his arms around them. "Thank fuck!"

Mina enveloped him in a trembling embrace. "Thank you," she managed to say between hoarse sobs.

"I'm getting her inhaler.?" Rochelle sped off in the direction of Mina's study, not waiting for an answer.

Thomas raced toward the wounded man. "Ray, the women are fine. Get Becky immobilised. My people are here."

Ray glanced at Mina. "Where's Lullu?"

"She got away. Probably hiding in the stables."

Ray gripped the cuffs from Thomas and restrained Becky's hands behind her back before standing, nodding toward the man he'd shot.

"He's alive. Good shot," Thomas said.

Rochelle returned with Mina's medication and assisted her in taking three large gulps of Ventolin.

"I need to find my daughter." Ray handed Thomas the rifle and ran out in to the night.

"Wait for me!" Mina called after him when two more shots echoed off the walls of the house.

Ray spun around and found Thomas kneeling over Ben. He was pressing both hands down on the man's chest as a chopper flew low over the house and sirens blared outside.

"Ben!" Mina sobbed.

"That little shit! I thought he was unconscious." Thomas motioned with his head toward Klein Piet who lay motionless, a rose blooming on his chest.

"He took aim at Mina. I got him, but Ben threw himself in front of the girls." Thomas shook his head.

17

Ray rolled onto his side. Early morning fingertips of warm sunshine found their way through the half-open curtains and stroked his beloved's face.

In the month that followed the farm attack, Ray had been exonerated from both the drug charges and the shooting incident. He'd almost finished the program at Redemption and already applied to study Marine Biology through an online university.

Things were looking up. He and Mina were back together, and Lullu had come through the ordeal relatively unscathed, many thanks to Vestra.

Mina groaned as she snuggled up to him. Her naked body rubbed against his.

Ray lifted his head and looked to the bedroom door. It was still closed and locked. They'd had to do that, as Lullu had a habit of interrupting them at the most inopportune times. For reasons Ray couldn't fathom, his daughter didn't know how to knock—but he loved that the worst problem in his life was his kid not knocking before entering.

"There's only one way to wake up a sleepyhead," he whispered as he slipped beneath the blankets and began planting kisses all over Mina's body, starting at her collarbone, nipping the hardened buds on her breasts, and making his way down her belly and finding his favourite spot—between her legs.

"Ray ..." She moaned sleepily as her hands reached down and gripped his hair.

He slid a finger between her lips ... God, she was always so ready for him.

Keeping the plump lips parted, he stroked her with the tip of his tongue. She groaned louder and arched her back. He drew his tongue up and down as he slid two fingers inside of her.

"Raaay ..." she mewled, and he smiled, wrapping his arms around her thighs as he made love to her with his mouth. The scent of her ecstasy drove him wild as she climaxed, her back arching, her hands pulling him up to her.

"Taste." His voice was hoarse as he kissed her.

"I want more," she murmured.

"Of course you do, baby." He positioned himself at her entrance and teased her with his hard, wet tip.

"God, Ray, pleeeease." Her eyes fluttered open, and Ray fell into their depths as he plunged deep inside of her.

Their rhythm quickly became frantic and rough as she raised her legs up and clenched his arse.

Ray threw back his head as she bit the skin on his collarbone, and they came.

———

"Moooommy, Daaaaddy! Will you please hurry up?" Lullu called from the house to where Ray and Mina stood at the edge of the hill, looking out over the ocean. Behind them, a brand-new wooden bench decorated the once lonesome area.

They started most mornings off standing or sitting here. A little out of respect, but mostly to remember that they lived in paradise.

The bench, which Ray had made by hand, was for Ben. On its back was a large copper plaque. Ray had hated the man until Ben had given his life for Mina.

In memory of Benjamin Meintjies
Friend, protector, hero

Ray traced his finger over the engraving, as Lullu called to them again.

"Coming." Mina turned and waved.

"Don't we only have to leave in half an hour?" Ray gave her a confused glance.

"Oh, you still have much to learn about your daughter. Especially on a comp day." Mina chuckled.

It was Lullu's vaulting competition for national colors. The girl had been almost impossible for most of the week. Ray really looked forward to spending the day with his pa, Rochelle, Thomas, and Mina's mom—one happy family at last. But his nerves were wrecked.

"How the hell do you cope with the stress? I don't know if I can watch our daughter do this." He took her hand in his.

"Well, I'll tell you one thing. I'm happy to be doing this with you for a change!" Mina chuckled as they walked inside, grabbed their bags and the car keys, and walked out the front door.

"Hurry up, you two slow pokes." Lullu hung out the back window of the large SUV that towed the horse trailer.

They hit the road. The comp was being held at a prestigious breeding farm a few hours' drive from Redemption.

Lullu donned her earphones and closed her eyes. Ray gave Mina a WTF look.

"She listens to Guns N' Roses. Says it helps her get her mojo on."

Ray simply shook his head. "The Gunners, of all bands. Thank God she has good taste."

"So, you given any thought to my offer?" She placed a hand on his jean-clad leg as he steered the vehicle toward the main road.

"Yeah. I can help out, but I think you have a winner in Vestra. She'll make a great manager alongside you.

I'm willing to do the hardcore shit like Ben used to, to keep the inmates in line. I don't mean to be ungrateful and I need the money, but I can't promise you all my time if I get accepted into my course." He shrugged.

"I understand. Any more news from Thomas?" She squeezed his knee, and he jumped a little. "You know I'm ticklish and I'm driving."

A cheeky grin was plastered across her face. "Pity the daughter is in the car today."

Her words elicited a memory from a few days before when she'd gone down on him while he drove them into town.

"Aaaah, baby. Now my jeans are all tight." He shook his head and smiled.

"Getting back to reality here." He removed her wondering hand from his thigh. "Yes. So, Thomas told me Cyril was a plant. They found the real Cyril shoved into an old oil drum. The fake Cyril was the one who planted the drugs to get me out of the way. He was the one who got hold of your security system and fed information to Becky and Klein Piet, who then gave it to Marnus."

"Fuckers!" Mina folded her arms across her chest.

"I hope they rot."

"Well, Becky's been admitted unconditionally to the psych ward of the prison. Apparently, she's not coping well with the death of her brother. As for Cyril and Marnus, they're locked away in some dark hole with the promise of a small window if they giv

Interpol the information needed to bring down the ring of smugglers."

A single tear snuck down Mina's cheek and she quickly wiped it off her face. "Ben didn't deserve to die."

It was Ray's turn to put his hand on her leg. "No, he didn't." And he meant every word.

———

It WAS ALMOST nine o'clock when they pulled in to their allocated parking spot on the breeding ranch.

Mina stretched as her feet hit the dirt.

"I'll be okay. See you inside." Lullu eagerly led her horse out of the trailer and greeted the groom allocated to her. Drina pulled up behind them.

"Hi. You ready, Lullu?" The trainer walked up to her prodigy.

"Sure am. We're gonna kick arse," Lullu replied.

"Lullu ..."

"Marie van der Westhuizen ... I know. Sorry, Ma. But we are!" Lullu sassed.

Mina and Ray walked up to her pulled her and Boesman into an embrace.

"Good luck. We love you," Mina said.

"And are so proud of you," Ray added

"ay, okay, I know." She waved them off and
piciously at Ray, who blushed and trotted
rse, Drina, and the groom.

"What was that about?" she asked, but Ray only shrugged.

"Thank goodness she's up second. It's the waiting that gets to you," Mina said as they entered the large dome—an indoor arena, like those seen on television.

"This must have cost a pretty packet," Ray said.

"Yup. American investors apparently," Mina replied as they found their seats and the rest of the family.

"Hi! I'm so glad you could all make it," Mina greeted Derek and her ma on her right-hand side, and Rochelle and Thomas on Ray's left.

"Great seats, eh? Usually we're right at the back." Her ma pointed out.

The first contestant walked in with a dapple-grey mare at her side. The judges gave her the go-ahead and she began. Her gymnastic moves caused everyone to suck in and hold their breaths.

"She'll be hard to beat," Mina whispered to Ray when Lullu walked in with Boesman. Dressed in her new bright purple and black outfit, Lullu positioned herself to wait for the starting signal from the judges.

Lullu worked through the routine she and Drina had practiced, with spectacular form.

"How's she doing?" Ray whispered, his grip on her hand tightening with every move.

"Great. I can't believe how much she's impr—oh my God!" Mina clapped her hand to her mouth as the crowd jumped to their feet and applauded so loudly, Mina's eardrums thrummed.

"She's just pulled off the technical roll." Mina applauded proudly when their daughter successfully completed the summersault roll off the neck of the horse and bowed to the crowd.

Ray pushed out his chest and let off a resounding whistle. "That's my daughter!" He turned and called out to the spectators around them, who congratulated them.

It was a nightmare having to sit through seven more performances, knowing how well Mina had ended hers But at last, all the riders and their horses rode back into the rink and lined up.

Scores were presented from lowest to highest, with the judges leaving the final three alone in the rink.

"She's made it to the top three!" Drina, who was seated behind Mina. squeezed her shoulders and squealed.

Everyone held their breaths, and only the swish of horse tails and snorts could be heard as the judges called out second place—the dappled mare and her rider.

"And the national colours are awarded to..." the announcer paused and the entire arena held their breaths, "Mina Van Der Westhuizen! With third place going to..."

The crowd erupted in more applause.

Lullu jumped up, standing on Boesman's back and bowed, then hopped off and bowed as the judges presented her with her ribbon and her colours.

Their family rose in unison, clapping and proffering wolf whistles. The rest of the crowd joined in. Tears streamed down Ray's eyes and the family laughed and celebrated. Mina closed her eyes, wanting to imprint this day on to her heart forever.

Lullu stood on her tippy-toes and whispered something to the lead judge, who nodded and smiled brightly.

Her daughter mounted Boesman and cantered smartly over to where they all sat in the front row. The horse stopped, and Lullu jumped up, standing once again on her horse's back.

"What the heck is she up to?" Mina asked as Ray stood, leaned over and took a box from his daughter, then turned to face Mina as he kneeled.

The entire crowed "aaahed" as Boesman followed suit and kneeled, and Ray opened the small black box.

"He will admit he was afraid," Lullu said out loud.

"But love returned and it did hold," Ray recited.

"His heart will play no games, I made him swear," Lullu continued.

"For it knows my name." Ray popped open the box.

Lullu finished, "And his true desire."

"I wrote this poem Mom." Lullu added, eliciting soft laughter form those who could hear.

Ray shook his head and returned his attention to Mina. "I loved you once; I love you still. I honestly hope that you might too?"

A heavy silence enveloped them as the arena

awaited a reaction from Mina, whose world was spinning off its axis.

"This was my ma's." His eyes shone like sapphires in the night sky. "And I would love for it to belong to you now. Mina van der Westhuizen, will you marry me?"

Mina glanced over his shoulder to where Boesman now stood up with Lullu sitting on his back. Her daughter smiled broadly as she nodded.

Mina looked to her ma and then to Derek, who both nodded and smiled, then back to Ray, who turned the colour of sour milk.

"Of course I will. I just wanted to make you poop your pants first."

They all burst out laughing.

She allowed Ray to slip the onyx and diamond white-gold, princess-cut ring on her finger before he wrapped his arms around her and held her tight.

The entire crowd applauded with quite a few wolf whistles and whoop-whoops in addition.

———

It was dark and late by the time Ray pulled up to the stables at Redemption. He cut off the engine but kept the headlights on. Mina and Lullu both sat sleeping in their seats.

Ray reached back and brushed a loose strands of hair that fell across his daughter's face. A year ago, he'd never have believed he'd be here. Back in the arms of his only love with his daughter. He'd never have believed that forgiveness was possible or that he'd ever deserve it. But here he was, on the verge of getting married, and a part of this gorgeous girl's life.

"You're my everything," he whispered as a hand touched his arm.

He looked back to Mina, who looked at him with so much love and acceptance his heart burst. "And so are you, baby. So are you."

He turned and leaned forward, kissing her like he'd never kiss her again.

AUTHOR'S NOTE

I'm sure if you've read *Simple Truths*, you'd have been super surprised that Ray gets to feature in his own love story. But Raymond Le Roux spoke to me early on in the process of creating his sister's story. I always knew there was more to him than his arsehole racist persona. I saw a damaged man. A young boy scared out of his wits and coping with a situation the only way he knew how. A situation no kid or human should ever have to find themselves in—and how that trauma followed him in to adulthood.

Again, I've shown you little bits of South Africa's truths, such as the poaching, human trafficking and the ever rampant farm attacks.

I also used a lot of artistic licence when describing the abalone farm because I wanted it to look a certain way. I also wanted to show how lucrative and sought-after abalone is.

Then I mentioned a man who re-created genuine seawater. He is someone I know from South Africa. He has a passion for sea life and discovered that all sea water had to be pumped in and refreshed from the ocean, so he spent millions of Rands and hours on developing fake seawater that had the same genetic make-up of real seawater. Unfortunately, for legal reasons, I can't mention names.

Tatensrope is an anagram for the town of Paternoster on the west coast of South Africa. I wanted a town that already existed, but also was my own.

Load shedding happens all the time in South Africa as the corrupt government have bankrupted municipalities and the electricity provider—therefore, not enough infrastructure upgrading has been able to take place and so not enough electricity is generated for a growing population.

A desert rose is a sand rose. It is found mainly in the Namib desert but is found on the west coast too. From the way the sand shifts and the morning dew soaks in to the sand, it freezes into a pattern looking almost exactly like a rose in full bloom. This story is written from a lot of life experience, chatting with people who've dealt with similar issues and because – SOUTH AFRICA!

To every human who's made good on their second chance—good on you. To those who have received one —it's worth the hard work. To those who've abused theirs—shame on you.

And last but most certainly not least – to a very special young lady who inspired Lullu's love for and brilliant accomplishment in the vaulting arena's of South Africa, **Chamonix Lombard** – always follow your dreams my girl, always!

Prelude

The clinic at the far north end of the Koinadugu District in Sierra Leone is busy, sticky, zooms with flies, and reeks of death. Another outbreak of Cholera in the small, poverty-stricken village has all the staff of our deployment of Doctors Without Borders at their wits end.

The canvas walls of the tent billow as hot wind slaps them to and fro, bringing little relief but only adding to the misery of life. My guide and self-proclaimed protector, Max, holds back the flap of the door for me to step out and stand beneath a threadbare tarp tied between two dead stumps. It provides little relief as a makeshift shield from the sun. In the distance, a herd of goats bleat when a lone bull dares to drink from the same trough that they do. The shade, distributed to them by trees I've never bothered to learn about, is sparse and practically nonexistent; here leaves, like people, wither as soon as they bloom.

"Dokta!" a rickety, parched voice calls out.

I look to my left as I duck and step out into the scorching African morning.

A woman, small in stature but strong in presence, walks toward me. Her grey hair is plaited in a way that pulls the skin of her face in tight lines around her eyes. Around her neck, wrists, and ankles hang leather straps decorated with feathers, stones, and beads. Her tan-colored three quarter pants and blue button-up top are well worn, but clean. Over her shoulder hangs a handmade leather bag decorated in beads and more: small bones. A bag I know from experience holds specially engraved bones, teeth, and other paraphernalia used by her kind.

"Be gon wit ya, woman!"

Max the ever loyal, steps forward and puts himself between the woman and me.

I tuck a wayward strand of my thick blond mop behind my ear. "It's okay. She means no harm." I place a hand on his shoulder.

"Aye, she be da devil with dem eyes."

"Shh, Max," I plead. "How can I help?" I ask, trying not to focus on her gaze. Her eyes, one blue as the sky crowning our heads and the other as brown as the darkest chocolate ever tempered are the mark of a witch, according to local lore.

I lower my gaze respectfully.

"I no be meanin ta bother." Her voice softens in a respectful tone as she apologizes and confirms my instincts.

Her skin is as leathery as her voice, but her body is strong. Her arms and legs, though slim, are lithe and toned, and her general appearance has no tell of the illness currently running rife through the village.

"Are you ill?" My hand instinctively rubs my tummy as I'm not sure why else she'd be here.

The woman throws her head back, and a cackle cracks like a whip through the heat-drenched air. Her laughter ceases as suddenly as it begins, and the woman inches closer.

Max tries to stand between us, but I shake my head as she reaches out and pinches my chin between her forefinger and thumb. She smells of smoldering fire and tobacco as she pins me to the spot with her mismatched gaze. For a moment, I am lost in the swirl of blue and brown.

"Noh, Dokta. I be free from da bad juju of dis place. But tis yew I cum ta see."

Her words carry no threat of harm or dreaded curses - not that I believe in curses - but the look in those eyes almost bring me to my knees.

Available for purchase here:

https://michelledaltonauthor.com/books/simple-truths/

FORGET ME NOT
LOST & FOUND - BOOK TWO

Prelude

Queensland in February is like sitting in a sauna with all your clothes on.

Isabella Irish flapped her T-shirt to and fro, hoping to create some airflow and cool off. She came to stand beneath the blooming poinciana tree which created a canopy over the open-air stage. The popular Eumundi Markets were as crowded on a Wednesday as they were on Saturdays. It'd been months since she'd visited the busy Sunshine Coast bazaar. Her stall, which had showcased her art, had sat not too far from where she was now—before Mark had secured her first break.

Two men and three women stepped onto the stage and

positioned themselves with their traditional indigenous instruments.

The earthy Australian music drifted out of a didgeridoo and flowed through her body, the player's circular breathing imitating the rain and the wind in his songs of the earth and the sky.

A hand drum soon joined in and Issi found herself carried away to a distant place as she rode the rhythm and sound of the song.

The fog which always clouded her fractured cognizance lifted, and a clarity she had not experienced since the terrorist attack, seeped into her damaged brain. She closed her eyes and shut out the hustle and bustle around her, enjoying the brief reprieve from a mind which had lost so much.

A deep bassy tone emanated from the instrument as the player worked the mouthpiece with his breath. The sound painted a picture of the elements, and kangaroos hopping across a vista—*boing, boing*. A third instrument joined in, adding a crispness like dry grass brushed by the wind . . . It drew her away from the present and into an open space of land, her heart echoing the beat of the drum. Reds and golds unfurled around her. The music drew her back to an ancient time . . .

"Hey. You enjoying the music?" Jeff leaned in with his chin on her shoulder.

"Geez!" Issi slapped a hand to her chest as she jumped.

"Sorry, lovely." He proffered a handsome smile along with his apology.

"Yeah. It tells a story if you listen closely." She returned the gesture to show him she was okay. "Where's Sam?" She leaned past Jeff. "I can't see him," she asked her ridiculously tall friend.

"Two rows down. He's discovered a stall that sells exotic food and art." Jeff rolled his eyes. "And I swear the stallholder's accent is just like yours."

"I don't have an accent." Issi waved off Jeff's odd comment. For a born-and-bred Australian, she sounded nothing like one. But her different way of pronouncing words, according to the specialist doctors, could be due to her acquired brain injury.

"Come. We need to save that man from himself. I can see him buying a truckload of foreign foods I know I won't eat. I mean, what in the holy heck is *paap*?" Jeff's lips tried to wrap themselves around the foreign word. The outcome was hilarious and Issi bit back her laughter.

He slipped an arm through hers and guided her to where Sam stood tasting food and peppering the short, plump stallholder with questions.

"Are you still tasting?" Jeff nudged his partner, who nodded and swallowed.

"This *pap* is good once you put some honey in it," he replied.

"What is it exactly?" Issi pointed to the bowl of what looked like bleached polenta.

"*Haai*. Why don't you know what pap is?" The woman's astonished expression caused Issi to pause.

Taking a step away from the table she shook her head.

"It's a maize porridge." Sam graciously drew the vendor's attention back to him. "Really, you both need to broaden your palatable horizons." He winked at Issi.

"*Ja*. So this is Achar," she said, glancing at Issi once or twice more. "And you can eat it with a lot of stuff, especially wif your *p-ah-p*." She pronounced the word slowly. "It gives it this really *lekka* . . . erm, *wat is nou die word vir smaak* . . . taste. *Ja*, taste! I make it from mango, curry . . ."

"Okay your accent isn't quite like that, but it shares a similarity. Even she thought you were a South African," Jeff whispered teasingly into Issi's ear, but she barely acknowledged him.

An uncomfortable sensation made itself known, as though someone had wrapped a lasso around her midriff and was tightening it with every passing moment. Disembodied voices fought to break free from the shattered fragments of her broken brain. She'd understood the woman's foreign words—but how? And then she spotted the easel standing center to the background of the stall. On it, an artwork . . .

A familiarity Issi couldn't put her finger on filled her head and stirred something in her heart. The style, she knew it . . . but like the foreign words spoken by the stallholder, she was not sure how.

She rubbed the scarred skin behind her left ear. The part of her brain devastated in the bomb blast ached, pleading with her to access what she had lost. Instead, nausea roiled in her belly and left her mouth dry and her vision blurred. Issi instinctively reached out and gripped Jeff's shoulder as her world turned.

"Lovely, are you okay?" Jeff stroked a stray lock off her cheek as Sam came to stand beside her.

"You're white as a sheet. Getting another migraine?" Sam rubbed a caring hand on her back.

Issi nodded, then pointed to the artwork. "How much?" was all she could get her stupid mouth to articulate.

Available for Purchase here:

https://michelledaltonauthor.com/books/forget-me-not/

OTHER BOOKS BY AUTHOR

Available for purchase here:

https://michelledaltonauthor.com/books/

ABOUT THE AUTHOR

G'day, howzit, sanibonani, goeie dag.

My readers know me as Michelle Dalton and my friends, as the call-a-spade-a-spade-South-African.

Originally from Pretoria, South Africa, Michelle Dalton and her family fled the rising violence taking over her beloved country and now lives near Brisbane, Australia with her husband and triplet sons.

While juggling a nursing career and teenage sons, she loves to escape into her fictional world. Michelle has a deep love of horses and enjoys weaving them into dramatic stories with honourable men and strong women.

Her other hobbies are gardening (usually trying to save her precious herbs and bulbs from an overactive miniature Jack Russell), painting, and reading. She's also a huge Star Trek and Marvel Comics fan, and as of recently a wee fan of DC too.

YOU CAN CONNECT WITH MICHELLE HERE:

HTTP://MICHELLEDALTONAUTHOR.COM

https://www.facebook.com/MichelleDaltonAuthor

https://www.instagram.com/michelledaltonauthor_/

https://www.pinterest.com.au/daltonauthor/_saved/

CPSIA information can be obtained
at www.ICGtesting.com
Printed in the USA
LVHW022040131020
668706LV00001B/321